Doorways to the Unseen 5

6 Tales of Terror and Suspense

James Dermond

Ambages Books

ISBN: 978-1-946038-04-3

Cover art by Jeff Purnawan

"Her abode is concealed in the lowest recesses of a cave, wanting sun, and not pervious to any wind, dismal and filled with benumbing cold; and which is ever without fire, and ever abounding with darkness."

- *Metamorphoses*, Ovid

Contents

Something in the Walls

S tanding in the tiled entryway, Timothy firmly shut the front door behind him. He inspected the letter that had fallen through the door's mail slot, postmarked late last month. The letter, addressed to him, was from Eleanor Cooke, his stepsister, whom he hadn't seen since childhood. *What could Eleanor want now*, Timothy thought, *after all these years?* The mystery of the letter piqued his curiosity.

Timothy carefully slit the starch white envelope with an opener and read its contents:

Dear Tim,

I couldn't find your phone number or any other personal details among my mother's things besides this address. I hope this letter has gone to the right place and, assuming it has, finds you well.

You may think it strange for me to contact you after so many years of silence. I know we were never close, mostly because of my mother, but something happened recently that has brought me home again.

Rose is afflicted with late-stage dementia and can no longer live on her own. She's been moved to a nursing facility where she can be cared for, and I've taken conservatorship of her estate, including the family home. We played together in the yard there as children for several summers.

But this is why I write to you: I've found something of your late father's that is quite interesting. Even intriguing. I can't say what it is other than that you must see it in person.

Over these last few years, my mother couldn't maintain the house as well as she should have, so I'm having it fully renovated by a local contractor. We found a feature in the home's cellar previously unknown to me during the subsequent work. A feature your father most likely had knowledge of, based on what I found of his.

I'll be at 47 Grove Street during the daytime until renovations are complete, which the contractor estimates will be on May 27th. By the time this letter arrives, you should have several weeks to make the trip out of state and visit. But please call ahead so we can catch up and discuss your plans. Mother's home number is written on the back of this letter.

Cordially,

Eleanor

Timothy turned over the letter and saw a hastily written phone number. *I haven't seen Eleanor since we were probably ten years old,* Timothy mused as he picked up the phone to call. The phone rang for some time, but there was no answer.

I'll just head down there tomorrow after checking in with the office, Timothy decided, eager to uncover what his father may have left for him. *I don't want to waste any time... and I must see what's waiting for me.*

Picking up the phone again, Timothy called his brokerage. "Hello, Janice. I need to go out of town starting tomorrow. No, not too far. I'll be back on Monday. Please let David know he'll need to close the Sullivan property without me. And let him know I'll call Friday afternoon to make sure all went well."

I could make an offer on the home, Timothy considered. *The market there is hot right now. But I won't broach the subject until I get ahold of whatever Eleanor has gotten from Dad.*

Involuntarily shuddering for a moment, Timothy recalled his stepmother's antiquated, sullen house and her cold, often imperious manner. His memories of both were not good but, with the passage of time, he now held more impressions than actual recollections about the old place and Rose. But why had he suddenly become afraid? Timothy shrugged off the feeling and began to pack his suitcase for the following day.

The trip along the expressway was a short one. Timothy soon found himself leaving the metro's bustle for the quiet, leafy environs of a historic city south, steeped in the charm of a bygone era, nestled along a bay. He pulled his convertible sedan to the curb near a house on Grove Street, a two-story Georgian-style frame dwelling, unremarkable in such a storied neighborhood.

The house rested alone in a wide alcove, twin chimneys protruding from its gray shingled roof. An open plot of elm trees lay behind it. Parked against the street curb nearby were a utility pickup truck and a silver sports coupe, contrasting their owners' wealth and social status.

Walking up the path to the house, Timothy reflected that the front door's ponderous, old-fashioned knocker could be something out of *A Christmas Carol*, and he imagined the ghost of Jacob Marley speaking his name as he reached for the brass doorknob. Finding the door open, Timothy went inside, half expecting the knocker to form a face and call out to him.

Construction work was being done somewhere in the house. A hammer pounding wood echoed as Timothy closed the door with a thud. He peered down the long hallway stretching from the house's foyer, rooms branching off on either side, but there was no one in sight. Above the din of the laboring hammer, Timothy called out heartily: "Eleanor, it's me, Tim. I can't wait to see you! Are you there?"

A reply came from the parlor to the left: a woman's soft voice partly muffled by the noises in the house. "Yes, Timothy," the voice said. "Please, come into the drawing room. Make sure that the door is closed behind you."

Timothy saw a stylishly dressed young woman standing in the shadows near the fireplace as he opened the cracked door. The parlor's heavy lace curtains obscured most of the sunshine, but some daylight still filtered through the windows and onto the parlor floor, not reaching the room's corners. A folded pair of dark sunglasses and a glossy black portfolio were close at hand, both resting on a varnished wood table.

Eleanor smiled and stepped forward as Timothy shut the door tight, taking him by both arms. She leaned in to kiss him lightly on the cheek.

Surprised, Timothy rubbed the spot where Eleanor had given him a peck and then smiled in return. "We were just kids the last time we saw each other," he noted, his grin quickly morphing into a smirk. "But you're all grown up now. I wasn't sure what to expect."

Eleanor continued to smile but said nothing, her large, pale-blue eyes set against almost platinum hair—an icy blonde *femme fatale*.

"You've grown up as well, Tim," Eleanor replied after pausing to study his face, flirtatiously touching the side of his auburn hair. "The chubby boy from all those years ago turned out rather well. I'm glad you received my letter."

Timothy stood by a window and scanned the room in the half-light, the gilded portraits of Eleanor's forebears dominating the space. Eleanor took a seat on a sofa and asked Timothy to join her. "Please sit down," she said brightly. "We've so much to discuss."

"Yes, indeed," Timothy agreed as he complied with her request. "But why all the mystery about my father's effects?

4

In your letter, you wrote you had something of his I needed to see in person, so here I am."

"We can talk about that later, upstairs," Eleanor indicated, reaching to touch Timothy's arm again. "But what about you?" she inquired, her manner animated. "Are you married? Any children?"

Growing sheepish, Timothy turned away for a moment. "No, I've never been married," he replied dejectedly. "My work takes up so much of my time. But maybe the right girl will come along someday." Timothy suddenly hoped that Eleanor was interested in him. "And yourself?" he asked, cheering. "Do you have a husband and children?"

"No," Eleanor said flatly, her reply oddly terse. An awkward silence then developed between them.

"Anyway," she declared at last, "I've so much to tell you. But first, down to business. I want to show you what Mr. da Silva found in the cellar before visiting your father's room."

Eleanor led Timothy down narrow steps, the top of his head almost touching the low plaster ceiling as they descended into the cellar. The dark room was cramped and unfinished but conspicuous stained wood paneling had been installed along its walls.

Putting down a can of paint as Timothy and Eleanor stopped at the bottom of the steps, a stout, mustachioed man clad in overalls dusted off his palms and extended a greeting. "Fred da Silva," he said, shaking Timothy's hand vigorously. "Ms. Cooke told me you might be coming."

"Timothy Faber," Timothy replied. "It's good to meet you." Looking past Mr. da Silva into a shadowy nook at the back of the cellar, Timothy saw a hefty pile of broken clay bricks close by.

Is that what we've come down here to see? Timothy wondered as he scrutinized the debris. *It looks like they've discovered something unexpected down here.*

5

Eleanor stepped around the two men and stood by the shattered brick heap. "Fred found this brick wall after knocking out some plaster to enlarge the cellar," Eleanor explained without looking at either of them. "He then bore into the wall as it seemed to be blocking another room in the back. That's when we found the tunnel."

Coughing, Timothy stooped and investigated the dark recess. A stone passage was faintly visible through a gaping hole in the brick wall. The passage was wide enough to accommodate someone standing upright and it seemed that it might lead to somewhere beneath the house.

"I told Ms. Cooke that it's probably an abandoned smuggler's tunnel," Mr. da Silva offered, reaching into one of the pockets of his overalls. "This house was no doubt built two centuries ago, but here's the thing: this brick wall and its plaster cover were put in much later, even just recently."

Producing a gold lighter and a red and green cigarette pack, Mr. da Silva pulled out a loose cigarette to place between his lips. "Mind if I smoke?" he asked. "This house makes me nervous for some reason."

"No, go ahead," Timothy replied somewhat absent-mindedly as he squinted through the hole in the wall. As Mr. da Silva sparked a flame, Timothy noticed that his lighter was monogrammed with a bold *DS* on its engraved case.

"So, what are you going to do about this creepy tunnel?" Timothy queried as he turned to face Eleanor. "Can't you just seal it up again?"

"We could," Eleanor answered, "but Fred thinks the tunnel might make the house's foundation structurally unsound. We should at least find out what's back there first. Where the tunnel leads to."

The three of them stared at the aperture in the brick wall, an uneasy silence hanging in the air, the hole like an agonizing wound in the house itself.

"Tomorrow's another day, my friends," Mr. da Silva suddenly said, seeming to search the cellar for his paint can. "We can discuss what needs to be done in the morning. I need to close up shop and go home for the day." He nodded to Timothy as he put out his cigarette on a clay brick. "It was nice meeting you, Mr. Faber," he said, his smile weary but friendly. "Have a good evening."

Eleanor and Timothy watched as Mr. da Silva walked up the steps from the cellar, soon hearing a door close upstairs. "When did Mr. da Silva find this tunnel, Eleanor?" Timothy questioned. "Do you think he's right about it being used for nefarious undertakings, even if it was a long time ago?"

"I don't know," Eleanor replied distractedly, apparently unconcerned. "We found the brick wall and tunnel about a week ago. I sent you the letter right after discovering it, hoping you'd turn up soon.

"I then told Fred to ignore the tunnel and to keep working on the rest of the house instead. He started back here just today." Eleanor glanced away to the steps exiting the cellar. "Come," she said. "Let's go upstairs."

Leading Timothy to the master bedroom, Eleanor opened the spacious closet. She parted the hung clothes, reaching down as she did so. After rummaging through a woven canvas trunk on the closet floor, Eleanor produced a slim, worn leather journal. Timothy took it in hand and began leafing through its embrittled pages, each one yellowed and creased with age.

"Be careful, Tim," Eleanor warned as he slowly flipped through the pages. "I suspect this journal is as old as the house itself. I found it at the bottom of a trunk of your father's belongings soon after my mother went into the facility. Still, I didn't think much of it until Fred found the tunnel. Now it makes more sense."

"How so?" replied Timothy, gingerly turning a page. "This just seems to be a personal diary but written in parts, using several different languages."

"Keep going and you'll see," Eleanor insisted. "I think it's actually written in a composite language, something like Esperanto, but even earlier. There are words derived from Greek, Latin, French, German, and some other languages I don't recognize mixed in with numbers and symbols.

"And there are blank pages in the back," Eleanor said in a low voice, her expression momentarily inscrutable. "The last entries could even be transcribed in invisible ink. The author wanted whatever the journal describes to be coherent only to a select few."

Timothy turned to the journal's final page and then looked at Eleanor, perplexed. "The author... who do you think wrote it?" he asked hesitantly, baffled by the odd book.

"Elijah Cooke, my distant ancestor," Eleanor replied with almost unerring conviction, her eyes widening as her mouth formed into a broad grin. "The man who built this house. He made a fortune by shipping goods—maybe even contraband—into the plantation colonies and then used the money to fund this house's construction."

"But back to my point: what does this journal have to do with the tunnel downstairs?" Timothy questioned, his brow furrowing. "You said it all makes sense now after finding the journal. How are the two connected, other than both are discomfiting relics of the past?"

Without answering, Eleanor turned to crouch and reached back into the canvas trunk, taking what looked like a map from a sturdy iron box. She then gave the map to Timothy and put the box aside.

"Both the journal and this old map were in the metal box, the map folded up under the journal," Eleanor informed him, her tone eager, even slightly devious. "The box looks like it was locked at one time, but I was able to just open it. There's no key for the keyhole that I could find anywhere."

Timothy held the small paper map by its ends. It showed the outline of a network of labyrinthian tunnels. He was surprised that the aged map was still usable after so long and wondered if its fibers had been strengthened—with linen, perhaps, or flax.

"This map likely shows what was sealed off behind the brick wall," Eleanor said, her excitement obvious. "And, if so, the journal most assuredly describes what's hidden there.

"Fred believes there's another part of the cellar—below ground—but I think Elijah Cooke's lost treasure is buried somewhere in the tunnels sketched on the map. Long-standing rumors in provincial lore claim something was secreted away beneath the Elijah Cooke House. And I think we've found it."

"It could be anything buried under the house, Eleanor," Timothy countered, suddenly worried about his stepsister. "What makes you believe there's lost treasure here? This strange book could be anything as well: about alchemy, a kind of military code, or just pedantic gibberish."

"Elijah Cooke had dealings with smugglers, like I said—even pirates," Eleanor responded wryly, evidently irritated by Timothy's skepticism. "The pirates were supposed to have paid him in Spanish doubloons from the Caribbean. A cache of gold coins worth millions could just be waiting for us in those tunnels.

"The old man disappeared some years after the house was built," Eleanor continued, "after a deal with some of his less savory business associates—slavers, probably, or pirates—went sour. But the house has remained in our family for all these generations, to this day."

"If the treasure's there, why not just go for it yourself?" Timothy asked, fearful he had brought himself into a dangerous situation. "You haven't seen me in years. I might as well be a stranger. Why trust me?"

"I've no one else to trust," Eleanor replied firmly, no longer seeming buoyant. "It's as simple as that. And I thought your father might have told you something about the map in confidence."

"Never, Eleanor," Timothy answered. "No, not a word. Not that we ever spoke very much."

"Then you agree to help?" Eleanor asked, hopeful. "You'll help me? If there's nothing valuable there, we'll at least find out what's in those tunnels."

Timothy nodded, unsure but tempted by the allure of forgotten wealth just begging to be taken. *Who could say no?* Timothy reassured himself. *I can't.*

"Good," Eleanor said, once again upbeat. "Let's wait until Fred leaves tomorrow and then explore the tunnels. I'll bring flashlights and a lantern, and we'll take the map with us. Fred won't be back until Monday morning, so we have enough time over the weekend to find our fortune if there's one to be found."

Once downstairs, Timothy sat at the kitchen table and watched Eleanor take a can of coffee from the cupboard and then run water into the coffee maker from the faucet. Fresh coffee began to percolate, and Eleanor sat at the table to join him.

"It's so funny being back in the old house after all these years," Timothy remarked as Eleanor gazed at him affectionately. He then paused, as if uncomfortable for a moment. "You know," Timothy confessed, "there were some nights here, nights while you were away at boarding school, that still haunt me."

Eleanor looked at Timothy quizzically, an expression of concern on her face. "How so?" she said urgently. "You're not trying to confess some past abuse you've kept secret until now, are you, Tim?" Eleanor suddenly seemed sad, as if she were about to hear something she might have suspected about their childhood.

"No, nothing like that, Eleanor," Timothy replied hurriedly, upset by the suggestion. "I can assure you." Timothy then looked around the kitchen momentarily as if he was inspecting the room. "I've always had a certain unease about this place," he said at last, "as did Dad. As if there was something in the walls of the house."

Without saying anything, Eleanor got up and poured two cups of coffee before returning to the table with the steaming mugs. "What do you mean?" she then inquired pointedly before taking a sip from her cup. "Like rats?"

Timothy drank from his mug and then looked back to Eleanor. "No, something else," he said, his voice trailing off momentarily. "I could never quite explain it. If I didn't know any better, I could have sworn, more than once, that someone was behind my bedroom walls, moving around at night."

Eleanor took another sip from her coffee cup as if unsure how to reply. "I don't really have any sharp memories of the house," Eleanor declared, almost wistful. "But, then again, I can't even remember my own father. He died when I was very young, according to Mom; all I ever knew was your father, Tim. He was my real dad, as much as I had one."

Eleanor lightly touched Timothy's hand and seemed about to say something. Instead, she took the last sip of her coffee and moved from the table to put the empty cup in the sink. "Have a good evening, stepbrother dearest," she said from the open arc of the kitchen doorway, ready to depart. "I'll see you tomorrow morning, bright and early at eight o'clock. Be back here for the treasure hunt after Fred leaves."

After dinner at a restaurant, Timothy checked into his hotel, which was some distance from Grove Street. The sun was beginning to set through the half-closed window blinds as he unlocked the door to his room, casting shadows over a neatly done-up single bed.

Sitting down to undress, Timothy recalled his conversations with Eleanor that afternoon. Eleanor's mother had been largely absent from their lives after adolescence; even so, Rose had never seemed "quite there" to Timothy, even during his boyhood. Her demeanor had often been aloof when they were together with his father, as if she'd somehow resented his presence or even saw him as an intruder.

Night came but Timothy lay awake, hazily recalling one afternoon at the old house many years ago. He hadn't thought of what had occurred that summer day since it happened, but seeing Eleanor again brought the memory back. He turned onto his side and shut his eyes tightly, the images in his mind of himself and Eleanor now as lucid as they had been on that day in their youthful past.

Eleanor sat in the shade of a blooming magnolia in the house's yard, her hands resting on her knees. She wore her requisite wide-brimmed sun hat and dark sunglasses, always on whenever she ventured outside. Rose always insisted Eleanor remain covered up, the girl's milky complexion being quite sensitive (according to her).

Perched atop his bicycle's striped leather seat, Timothy rode along the sidewalk, Eleanor watching him coast past the house's white picket fence. Timothy abruptly lurched forward without warning and hurtled over the bike's handlebars onto the hard pavement with a clamor.

Eleanor shot up from her spot and scanned the front of the house, removing her sunglasses as she did so. Timothy staggered to his feet and opened the fence gate, forgetting his bike where it lay broken. He made his way to the house unsteadily, clutching a bloody elbow.

"Tim!" Eleanor cried out after watching the scene unfold, then ran to him from the sheltering tree and inspected the arm he was grasping. "You're bleeding," she observed. "Let me have a look."

She held Timothy's damaged arm with both hands. "How did it happen?" she asked as Timothy revealed a nasty gash across his left elbow. "You just went flying all of a sudden."

"I hit something; it got caught in the spokes," answered Timothy, wincing as Eleanor brought his arm closer to her face. "But I want to get some iodine on this cut before I find out what it was."

"Tim, your cheek's scraped pretty bad too," Eleanor said, her voice full of sympathy. She stood on the tips of her saddle shoes and kissed Timothy on the cheek in a place where he hadn't been hurt. As she stepped back, Eleanor saw a thin drop of blood forming in the open abrasion, as if poised to stream down Timothy's chin.

Almost unconsciously, she reached up to catch the droplet on her finger and then licked the fresh blood from its tip in one fluid motion. Timothy stared into Eleanor's face as he saw this, a perverse look of satisfaction now resting there.

"Why did you do that?" Timothy asked uneasily, putting a hand to the scrape as if to search for more blood from his injury.

"Do what?" Eleanor replied, apparently surprised at the question. "Oh, you mean... I don't know; it seemed the right thing to do."

Sleep eventually took hold of Timothy, and the night passed into the morning. Rolling over, Timothy squinted at the table flip clock's blocky white numbers, which read 9:27 a.m. He had slept in despite requesting a wake-up call from the front desk the prior evening.

"Why didn't I get a wake-up call?"

The young man behind the lobby's counter turned to see who was speaking to him. "I'm sorry, sir," he told Timothy. "What room are you staying in?" The hotel clerk tried to hide his irritation at Timothy's brusque manner but was entirely unsuccessful at doing so.

"I'm staying in Room 372," Timothy replied. "I checked in yesterday evening when a different person was behind the desk. Did I get a call or not?" Timothy waited for an answer, taking another gulp from his vending machine paper cup.

"You did, sir," the clerk said after checking a logbook under the counter. "I placed the call myself several hours ago. The phone rang and rang, but there was no reply. I apologize if there was any inconvenience."

His head dull and throbbing, Timothy drove back to where Eleanor was waiting for him (or so he hoped). He had phoned the house from his hotel room, but no one had answered. *Eleanor may have just been down in the cellar with Mr. da Silva,* Timothy thought to himself, then cursing his heavy slumber.

Why had he slept so deeply, failing even to answer a ringing phone beside his bed? *There was a nightmare last night after I finally fell asleep,* Timothy thought. *Something that put me down. But I can't remember what it was.*

The door to the house was unlocked again. As Timothy had expected, Mr. da Silva's truck and Eleanor's silver coupe were parked nearby. Once inside, he found two cups of coffee cooling on the kitchen table, having clearly been poured recently and then left unfinished.

So, they must be downstairs, Timothy thought. *That's why Eleanor didn't answer the phone. I just hope they didn't decide to go into the tunnels without me.* He walked down into the cellar, finding the space as it had been left the previous day—but empty.

Next to the brick wall lay Mr. da Silva's bag of tools, which he had left in the kitchen the day before. *It seems da Silva may have put the bag here so he could crawl through,* Timothy decided. *I'm glad I wore jeans for this.*

Timothy pulled himself into the exposed opening in the brick wall, the dark tunnel ahead. Running his hand over its walls after standing upright, Timothy saw that the tunnel's masonry work appeared much like the house above. Its stones must have been laid in colonial times, he decided. Timothy turned on the flashlight he had taken from da Silva's tool bag and stepped into the darkness, the solitary beam of light revealing the way ahead.

At the far end of the tunnel were piles of large rocks that looked as if they had been cleared away to make whatever was below accessible. The tunnel appeared to have been blocked with the worn mass of stones and then unsealed at some point, its reason untold.

The stone passage descended, quickly becoming earthen. Near the passage's bottom were yet more earthen passages leading in several directions. *Eleanor's map likely shows what's down here, but I don't have it*, Timothy reflected. *Should I turn around and call the police? No—they might be hurt, so I shouldn't waste any more time. I need to find them.*

The passage south was much deeper than Timothy had anticipated, and he continued for some time with no sign of Mr. da Silva or Eleanor. The passage then veered to what Timothy thought was east. He followed it downward until he noticed the glint of metal somewhere on the passage floor. It was Mr. da Silva's monogrammed lighter, its stylized "DS" visible only after Timothy had brushed off the dirt encrusting it.

They must be close, Timothy decided. *I just hope they're alright.* The eastern passage emerged into a chamber of sorts, its rounded corners partially filled with what appeared to be bones. At its far end, a figure was slouched in the dim light of Timothy's flashlight.

Upon examining the figure, Timothy found that the mummified remains were clothed, the poor unfortunate having been manacled to the chamber wall at the time of his demise. Timothy shone his light aside, spotting a pile of rags and broken chains lying within reach of the prisoner. A crudely hewn inscription was carved into the nearby wall's soft stone: the hopeless last words of a man drawing his final breaths.

So, I have been taken captive. The creatures that dwell here, cousins of Mankind from before our History, have acted with the aid of human conspirators in the hopes I might reveal where my Wealth has been sequestered away. I have told them nothing, so they leave me here to rot out of spite.

At first, I befriended the strange beings living here in this lightless place, hidden from Christ's Mercy. I learnt to speak their peculiar tongue, informing them of the world above this one. They slowly became more demanding, asking for meat. For flesh of the most repulsive variety. And captives. Women. For an unspeakable purpose I dare not discuss.

Had I realized the creatures' domain was under this plot, I would have never built my Manse here among the groves. My prayer to Our Lord is that these Ungodly Monstrosities be sealed off so no harm can come to His Servants now that they know of us.

A glimmer of metal beneath the rags reflected Timothy's flashlight beam. Parting the decomposing tatters with a foot, Timothy spied a small music box lying on its side.

Carefully, Timothy opened the bejeweled box. Its lid unlatched and a ballerina began to pirouette on her tiny pedestal, a sweet melody echoing in the otherwise silent chamber. Momentarily spellbound by the haunting cadence of the notes, Timothy's thoughts turned inward to the disturbing night terror from his sleep, a suppressed phantasm of a storm-swept night spent at the old house years ago.

The dim thumping in the walls had returned, prodding Timothy from his slumber. Timothy wasn't sure what he had heard the night before but, this time, it was clear. Something was in the walls, moving about behind the bed. Sitting up, Timothy heard the noises stop.

Lightning flashed outside the bedroom window and there was a clap of thunder. Timothy's father, Rupert, was again away on business. Timothy was alone in the house with Rose for a second night.

He had searched for Rose earlier in the evening, even checking the cellar door, which remained locked shut, as always. Assuming she was downstairs, Timothy went to bed despite the din from the terrible storm.

A jewel-encrusted music box rested on a dresser past the bed's footboard, its lid closed. Timothy roused himself and stood before the bedroom window, reaching up to take the music box as more thunder rumbled faintly in the distance. Opening the antique device, he peered down at the exquisite porcelain dancer posing in the box's center, soft music now chiming as the ballerina turned.

Teeming rain splattered the glass of the window. Timothy listened as he heard a door open from the floor below and then close. That sounded like the cellar door, *Timothy thought.* Why would Rose have been down there all this time?

He shut the box's cover and climbed back into bed. There were footsteps outside his door; they paused at the threshold. The footsteps then resumed, trailing off, their sound quieted by the tumultuous thunderstorm. His head on his pillow, Timothy drifted into sleep.

He soon woke again, the rolling waves of cracking and booming thunder pulling him into an uncertain wakefulness. Rose was at the foot of the bed, partially concealed by the hanging canopy. She stared at Timothy without uttering a word. The rank odor of rotted meat assaulted his nostrils.

A hunched form stood behind Rose in the darkness of the bedroom. It heaved in shallow, ragged breaths, the smell of its foul gasps acrid and pungent. A mercurial lightning streak revealed for but a moment something that appeared like an albino ape, and then the room once again was almost devoid of light.

With Rose, the creature turned to leave through the open door, the crashing tempest outside nearly shaking the house. The door to the bedroom closed behind them and Timothy fell back into sleep, his semiconscious mind unsure if what he had seen was real or yet another nightmare.

There was a noise from down the passage to the chamber, a yowl or the cry of a feral animal. Searching for an exit, Timothy noticed another tunnel leading away and took it.

He stumbled through the egress passageway, hearing more cries and wails behind him, the light from his flashlight casting over loose stones and aberrant footprints left in the dreck by this underworld's putrescent inhabitants.

The choked passages twisted and turned, one soon becoming indistinguishable from the next. The relentless primal yowling grew closer, almost palpable. Now Timothy was all but lost in this seemingly endless underground maze.

At the passage's end, he spied a glow in the distance, the kind of light that might come from a lamp. Timothy went to the light instinctively, his overpowering fright blotting out the reason for his descent into these accursed tunnels.

A lantern was set on the ground of an open chamber, its dim blue radiance illuminating a grisly scene not far away. Eleanor kneeled over Mr. da Silva's corpse, gobbling and slurping, her arched back turned away from Timothy.

As Timothy drew closer, Eleanor snapped around, her long silvery hair wild, her mouth and teeth smeared with bright red gore from da Silva's half-eaten face. She stood, her head low, and began slowly walking toward Timothy, the color of her eyes now a dull, grayish scarlet.

Timothy wanted to flee but was paralyzed with fear; he felt frozen, as if a great force was holding him in place. Sliding a crimson-stained hand under Timothy's chin, Eleanor leaned in as if to kiss his cheek.

Timothy's blood-curdling screams echoed off the walls of the subterranean passageways and tunnels, answered only by the primordial shrieks of Eleanor Cooke's bestial kindred.

The Dining Car at Midnight

*W*hat a miserable little town, Charles decided, grimacing as he noted the hovels around him. Having just left the ill-maintained docks where the ferry had deposited its fares, Charles was tired; it had been a long trip down the river.

He had walked some distance with his luggage before stopping and placing his suitcases down on the cobblestones of what appeared to be the town center. Charles saw that there were few other travelers thereabouts, the dusky locals conspicuous among any visitors due to their gaudy clothing and dubious manner.

Checking his suit coat for his ticket and then glancing at his pocket watch, Charles wondered how much time he had. *The train depot shouldn't be too far from here and I still have a few hours before departure. But I shouldn't want to eat lunch in this place.*

He picked up his suitcases by their handles and spied signage not far away. The signs were not in a language he could easily translate, but it was clear from the façade of the peeling building from which the signs dangled that this was the railway station.

The waiting train on the station's tracks consisted of seven cars and a locomotive with its attached coal bin, all of which were of contemporary design. Sleek and outwardly luxurious, the modern-day transport posed a sharp contrast to the environs of this sleepy, out-of-the-way burgh where it was now parked. After spending the last several months first at sea and then at an Oriental capital, Charles was pleased to see something recognizable, a reminder of the Pullman cars from his cross-country travels at home.

The connecting passengers must still be on the train, Charles thought as he stepped onto the mostly vacant station platform, momentarily excited by the notion of joining them onboard. *The next ferry won't dock until late this afternoon. This town isn't exactly welcoming to outsiders, so I don't blame them for staying where they are for now.*

An ominous-seeming carriage was pulled up not far from the railroad station, near to the train's rearmost baggage car, two charcoal-black horses hitched to its front. The four-wheeled carriage's style was that of a bygone era, antiquated, but with a velvety case and plush interior still richly textured and opulent. A flatbed wagon, also drawn by two horses, was being driven away nearby, leaving the train station and rolling over the cobbled streets.

Charles watched as the train's porters loaded a large wooden crate into the rear baggage car, struggling under its considerable weight. A gloved man wearing a felt bowler hat closely observed them. He then noticed Charles and shot him a bewildering smile. The man almost leered at Charles as if he were about to suggest something quite lurid to him.

Boarding the train, Charles handed his ticket to the assistant conductor, who waited at the car's passenger entrance. He was directed to his assigned sleeping accommodations, where he would ride in a single compartment.

Charles noted the compartment's darkly elegant lacquered wood and inlaid marquetry as he opened its door. A small washstand was near the berth, which was folded into a seat for the time being. *The splendor of this train compares to that of the finest hotels*, Charles reflected, *either at home or abroad.*

A three-course lunch was being served in the dining car. Charles strolled to the restaurant, finding the train somewhat empty considering its lengthy cross-border trek back to its home station. The *maître d'hôtel* greeted Charles as he stood at the dining car's threshold, his trim mustache wrinkling as he inspected his latest guest.

"Will you be dining alone, *Monsieur*?" the head waiter inquired, an inkling of derision in his tone. "There are tables for solo travelers, or you may sit with the other passengers if you wish. Our entrée this afternoon is *poulet à la chasseur*, with oysters as the appetizer."

Looking around the partially unoccupied coach, Charles noticed an older couple seated nearby. The man noticed Charles with the waiter and waved him over as if encouraging him not to dine alone.

"I will sit with the man and his lady if you don't mind," Charles replied, gesturing toward the distinguished pair. "They seem to want company."

"You shouldn't have to eat all by yourself," the man said as Charles sat across from him. "We've plenty of room here. We were just about to order lunch." He smiled genially at Charles, his wife smiling as well but staying silent.

"My name's Charles Hubbard," Charles said, extending his hand to greet the man. "I'm a senior correspondent for *The Daily Sentinel* newspaper. We're planning to open an overseas news bureau later this year. I'll be the new bureau's first editor-in-chief."

The man shook Charles' hand earnestly. "Sir Andrew Saxton," the man said in reply. "And this is my dearest wife, Winifred. We're on our maiden trip aboard this new luxury line. Isn't it just exquisite?"

"Yes, I'm quite impressed," Charles remarked as his eyes searched for a waiter. "Even more so as my employer is footing the bill for all of this. But why didn't you offboard for the ferry at our last station?"

"Winifred and I haven't left the train since our departure last week," Sir Andrew answered. "We're getting on in years and didn't want to traverse the final, rough part of the journey by boat. What I really wanted to see was this region, as steeped in history as it is."

Charles suddenly became curious. "Really? How so? I thought this place had always been a backwater, removed from most of the great events of the past."

"Not quite," Sir Andrew corrected. "Kings and queens have graced these remote lands; an order of crusading knights even kept a garrison here. That is, before their grand master was burned at the stake for heresy, among other things."

"Heresy?" Charles inquired, his curiosity whetted. "Like what? Did he deny the existence of God or something?" Charles found the notion a quaint one.

"No, not entirely," Sir Andrew said, the timbre of his voice lowering as he spoke. "The grand master was purported to have claimed that he was a half-daemon and that, through the ritual drinking of human blood, he would someday fully attain eternal life, even godhood.

"But he and his order were put to an end by the king. He was said to have cursed the king and his line before his execution by fire, pledging to someday rise from the grave, restore his order, and take his revenge against those who had wronged him. The grand master's surviving acolytes were then reputed to have spirited away his charred remains following his immolation by royal decree."

Surprised by this macabre turn in the conversation, Charles was startled when a waiter approached their table and asked if they wished to order lunch. Charles said yes but wanted to hear more from Sir Andrew before he ate anything.

"This curse, did anything ever come of it?" Charles was almost starting to give credence to this story; Sir Andrew was so convincing.

"Yes, if the legends are to be believed." Sir Andrew now wore an enigmatic expression across his face. "The king who sentenced the knights and their master to a fiery death died himself soon after. The king's death was supposed to have been a hunting accident, but from the accounts of witnesses, the king died of a terrible fright."

Lunch came and Charles took a small bite from his cooked chicken after slicing a piece off with his table knife. Sir Andrew and Winifred, still silent, ate the same meal. Charles' curiosity concerning this esoteric knightly brotherhood hadn't waned. He asked, "Does this order still exist? I mean, do you know if the heirs of those knights have a fraternal society today?"

"I believe they may," Sir Andrew replied, his voice strangely quiet. "But if the order continues on, its members maintain themselves in secret."

There was an uneasy break in the conversation following this remark, with Sir Andrew suddenly excusing himself. "I'm going to take a cigar on the vestibule. It was good meeting you, Mr. Hubbard. I hope we meet again soon." Sir Andrew stood and walked away.

Winifred offered an almost whispered goodbye to Charles as she followed her husband out of the dining car.

Charles sat alone for the remainder of his meal, then rose and entered the vestibule where Sir Andrew had stood only moments ago, briefly glancing at Charles' table through the open doorway before slipping off. The aroma of cigar smoke still hung over the now empty space, its distinctive fragrance sharp and sweet. Charles ambled toward his compartment near the back of the train, intent on getting some writing done prior to dinner.

It was night, the evening having come sooner than expected. Charles sat alone in his compartment, watching the night-time forest's densely knotted boles pass by his window under the moonlight. The train had left what little civilization existed in this part of the world, journeying into a yawning woodland darkness.

Charles had started drafting what would eventually be a multi-part article for *The Daily Sentinel*, covering his recent transcontinental adventure and the politics of the foreign country he had visited. *The Mustafa hopes to pull his hidebound compatriots into this century*, Charles mused to himself, putting away his journal and writing pen.

The hour was late, but Charles decided to venture outside his compartment and visit the adjoining baggage car now that the mystery cargo from earlier in the day had been hoisted into it. He thought back to the unsettling man on the station platform and his weird, unnerving smile.

I wonder if the crate has been pried opened by the porters. I'll bet they're as curious as I am about the thing. Charles stood in the narrow passage outside his compartment and made his way to the rear car's gangway connection. He paused for a moment in the tight vestibule, his hand hovering over the baggage car's iron-bound door, before heaving it open.

A hanging lantern swayed from the car's arched ceiling, casting eerie shadows about the crowded freight room as Charles teetered under the train's movement. Heavy boxes lined the walls of the car, scores of passengers' luggage flanking a tapering path that ended at a bulky crate toward the car's back.

Charles stopped in front of the crate and looked up, examining its sides. Unfamiliar script was stamped along the crate's wood surface. Some numbers near its top seemed to indicate a shipping schedule. Reaching out to run a hand over the crate's paneling, Charles abruptly pulled back once he touched his palm to its surface.

The crate is so cold... unnaturally cold, Charles thought as he shivered, warming his chilled hand in a coat pocket. *Feels like it's been left outside all winter.* As Charles looked around the car, he noticed his breath had begun to frost, revealing a thin mist as he nervously exhaled.

The train car shifted unexpectedly and the ponderous crate groaned, sliding slightly along the floorboards. Charles felt a shadow behind him, the tenebrous form's drawn fingers seeming to reach toward him as it grew longer, stretching over the crate.

Charles turned and the shadow receded, with only the sounds of the creaking lantern and the train clattering on its track remaining apparent. Afraid, Charles began to hurry towards the car's door when he heard a noise outside in the vestibule.

Entering, he saw the back of a man in a funereal coat and hat pulling shut the door to the connecting passenger coach. Charles stepped forward and the man turned to him, surprised. It was the man in the bowler hat from the station platform.

"Sir, what is your business in the luggage compartment at this hour?" the man queried, his voice as unpleasant as his visage. "You should be in your room, asleep."

"I could ask you the same, sir," Charles replied with some menace. "Now, let me be on my way. Please, step aside."

The two men passed each other in the compact space, wary and facing one another. Now that Charles was close, he could see that the man had a bloodless complexion, with bruised circles under both of his eyes.

The man leered at Charles again for a moment as he passed and then quickly busied himself with the door to the baggage car. From the corner of his eye, Charles saw the man close the baggage car door behind him as he exited the vestibule.

Returning to his sleeping quarters, Charles rested on the open berth after hanging his necktie. The light in the compartment slowly dimmed and Charles drifted into a languid slumber, lulled to sleep by the vacillating motion of the moving train.

He dreamed of a bleak and inhospitable place, barren and desolate save for a black fortress resting against the side of a jagged and broken mountain. Up a path to the mountain assembled a solemn procession: bearded men holding aloft banners and wearing tunics that displayed an inverted cross.

The procession entered the magnific stronghold, several of them carrying a bronze coffin to some resting place within. A horrifically burned corpse was removed from the coffin and lowered into a stone pool filled with blood, which soon restored what had once been a man to a semi-living state. The awful creature made a sinister laugh as it stood upright in the viscous crimson ichor, triumphant at having conquered death itself.

Drifting in and out of his fitful sleep, Charles felt intense, burning eyes on him before he finally awoke to the lightless compartment. He sat up on his berth and heard footsteps outside his door, noticeable in the otherwise quiet train.

Cautiously, Charles turned the compartment's doorknob and stepped into the hallway outside his room. It was empty. More footsteps echoed from somewhere at the end of the sleeping car's passage and Charles decided to follow them.

It may be that ghoulish man from the freight carriage spying on me, Charles concluded. *I won't let him get away!*

The footsteps continued until Charles reached the dining car. The door to the restaurant was cracked open. The sweet, sharp tang of Sir Andrew's cigar smoke wafted through the vestibule, seemingly from within the car itself.

Was it Sir Andrew then? thought Charles. *Perhaps a late-night snack?* But the dining car was as dark as the rest of the train at this hour.

The overhead gas lamps of the restaurant car seemed to light themselves as Charles entered. At each dining table were guests, men and women, all impeccably dressed for a formal occasion. They smiled all at once: their fangs bared, their lips ruby-red against white, cadaverous skin.

The door behind Charles closed silently and the guests rushed forward, swarming him, cutting off a scream of terror before it left his throat.

They fed voraciously on Charles' now still form, ceasing only after the last drop of blood had been consumed.

The porter knocked twice before unlocking the door to Charles' compartment with his key. "Is anyone here?" the porter asked heedfully as he turned the doorknob. "The train's stopped and you're the last passenger who hasn't claimed any baggage. You must disembark at this station."

Charles' drained and anemic corpse lay on the berth, its glassy eyes open and staring. The porter stood over Charles and decided that the man must have died in his sleep a few nights ago and that no one had noticed. But what was peculiar was that Charles was fully dressed—all except for his necktie.

Badcock's Tonic Bitters

"**C**ome one, come all! Come and see the amazing cure-all tonic, truly a miracle of modern medicine." As he spoke, Benjamin Badcock held aloft a bottle of bluish liquid, about the size of a whiskey flask, to allow the crowd to get a better look at his product. Dozens of townspeople had gathered around the raised stage in front of Badcock's horse-drawn wagon, gawking at the snake-oil salesman. A cloth-covered stand on the wood platform displayed four bottles in a line, with the sign underneath reading *Badcock's Tonic Bitters*.

The town of Tabletop was nestled among the foothills of a large and arid plane in the shadow of a mesa that overlooked the town. This barren rock formation provided shade to the town's inhabitants in which to shelter from the strong sun of the frontier, allowing the noon rays to be at least bearable. Badcock had rolled into Tabletop at around this time and had set up shop, new to the community.

Badcock scanned the faces before him. "You, young man," he shouted into the assembled throng, spotting someone toward the back. "Are you afflicted by any ailment? I saw that you limped as you walked to the stage. Do you have the gout?"

Tall and lean and wearing a cattleman's hat, the young man answered with some emotion: "I was thrown from a horse a while back and my leg's still not quite right. You're sayin' that your liniment can fix that?"

"Indeed, my good friend," Badcock replied, "indeed, I am. Please step up here and be the first to buy a phial of Badcock's Tonic Bitters at the knockdown price of only one dollar. Truly a bargain for such a wonderous concoction!"

The man in the back stepped onto the stage as the crowd parted, moving stiffly as he went. Removing a dollar from a billfold, the man handed it over and Badcock passed him a bottle from his display stand. The cattleman first took only a swallow of the elixir, followed by a gulp, and then the rest in one guzzle.

The man rubbed his bad leg and said, "I think it's gettin' better. It don't feel so sharp no more." He then began to walk around the stage more confidently until his limp disappeared after several steps.

"I'm cured!" the man exclaimed, ecstatic. "My leg's as good as new. This here tonic done did it!" He then slapped Badcock on the back, almost knocking off his barker's top hat, and beamed to the crowd from the stage.

The townspeople immediately rushed forward, waving dollar bills, vying to be the first to buy a bottle of the magic tonic. Badcock took an entire case of the stuff out from behind his stand, opened the box, and grabbed customers' dollar notes almost as quickly as they were handed to him.

"Remember, my good friends," Badcock announced as he sold the last bottle from the case, "the results may take some time. Give it a few days to cure what ails you. Badcock's Tonic Bitters is your one-and-only antidote for aches and pains."

Later, in the early evening, as the burned-orange sun set over the high desert prairie, Badcock drove his wagon to the outskirts of the town. The man in the cattle hat rested against a sparse tree in the twilight, the embers of a lit cigar revealing his presence in the semi-dark.

Badcock patted his horse's flank after dropping down from the wagon's seat. He walked to its back end past the stylized letters painted on its side, which read *The Medicine Show*. Reaching into the wagon, Badcock produced a paper box from which he took a stack of dollar bills. The cattleman was already at his side, waiting.

"Try not to topple the hat from my head next time," Badcock insisted as he handed his accomplice his cut of the take. "There was no need for all those theatrics."

"I jus' wanted to make it look real, that's all," the man replied, squinting as he counted the notes in the low light. "It looks like we made out this time."

"Yes, indeed we did," Badcock said, smiling in the dark. "We'll meet next in Cortez, three days from now. Show up the day before as always so it's not too suspicious."

The cattleman grinned and pocketed his loot, tipped his hat, and then made his way toward a horse hitched to the nearby tree. Badcock climbed into the back of the wagon, inspecting his remaining cases of tonic. What he had in stock should last him for at least the next several towns on this trip, if not more.

Badcock's wagon rolled on over the solitary road out of town, a lone traveler on this otherwise deserted rocky pathway. There was a sharp snapping sound beneath him, and Badcock lurched forward in his seat. The wagon abruptly shifted to one side.

Damn, it's that wheel again, Badcock cursed to himself. *It might be broken for sure this time.*

Badcock let himself down from the lopsided wagon and strained his eyes in the moonlight. The spokes of one of the wheels in the back had caught something in the dark, splintering them and bringing his journey to a halt. The wheel's rim was wedged into the dirt, no longer capable of turning without intervention.

Letting out a sign, Badcock stepped off the pitted road and into the sparse grass beyond it, the occasional tree dotting the fields the only shelter. He unbuttoned the fly of his trousers and began to relieve himself against one of the trees, its leaves rustling softly in the nighttime breeze.

Whistling a tune as he faced the tree, Badcock failed to hear someone approach his wagon on the road from Tabletop.

"Turn around with your hands up, you no-good cheat," the thin, reedy voice commanded in short gasps. "You poisoned me with your charlatan's brew."

Slowly turning to face the road as he buttoned his pants, Badcock saw the silhouette of a man holding a revolver, the gun's barrel pointed at him. The bearded man slouched as he stood on the road, clutching his stomach with his free hand as if in pain; still, he managed to keep his gun trained on Badcock.

"Why, my good sir, I did no such thing," Badcock insisted with rehearsed sincerity, taking a step forward as he put up his hands. "I'm sure we can reach an amicable solution if you believe I've harmed you somehow. I'm more than willing to compensate you appropriately for any malfeasance."

"That's enough, not one foot closer," the old miner wheezed, his firearm shaking slightly. "What I want is an antidote if you got one. If you ain't got a cure, I'll shoot you where you stand. Your days a' sellin' quack remedies will be through."

"You must have had a bad reaction, that's all," Badcock assured the man, mentally calculating how quickly he could pull his pocket derringer from under his jacket sleeve once he drew near his assailant. "I keep a tincture of laudanum in the back of my wagon for just such a purpose. If you would allow me to fetch it for you..."

Keeping his hands in the air, Badcock motioned as if to take a step toward the wagon. The miner swallowed in agony and then waved his gun, beckoning Badcock to him.

"No tricks now; I've got you in my sights," the miner warned as he took aim again, his voice almost fading into an asthmatic cough with the last word.

Badcock relaxed his arms and reached for a small chest resting among some crates. The miner observed him carefully, his breathing shallow and uneven.

The chest did indeed hold a tincture of laudanum, but Badcock had no intention of sharing any of it with this dying fool. But before Badcock could take the chest in hand, the old miner was seized by a sudden spasm, his firing arm reflexively dropping to his side.

Seeing his chance, Badcock darted for the Colt derringer in its custom sleeve holster, seamlessly sliding the gun into his hand. The miner raised his head after doubling over and saw the gun fire, the bullet striking him squarely in the chest. He stumbled backward and fell, but not before firing a return round into Badcock's gut.

Badcock sank to the ground, leaning on the wagon's back. The dark sky above him grew blurred, but he could make out a man's face peering down at him.

"I wasn't sure if you were going to make it." The voice from the darkness sounded muffled to Badcock as if it was being filtered through a heavy gauze. "You were out for more than a day after I extracted the bullet. But you should recover in time."

The room was sunlit and it took a moment for Badcock's eyes to adjust to the sudden intrusion of daylight. He rolled his head on the pillow and saw what looked like the shelves of a surgery lined with glass jars, bandages, and other medicinal supplies. The man standing over Badcock appeared friendly, his avuncular mustache and gentle smile reassuring.

"I was shot," Badcock noted from his pillow, fatigued and still dizzy.

"That you were, my friend," his host affirmed, turning away to reach for something on a shelf. "But your disgruntled customer wasn't so lucky. Was he wanting a refund?"

"Not exactly." Badcock tried to sit up on the surgery table but then felt a stabbing pain in his midsection. He lay back down, resting on his back, eyes meeting the unlit gaslight lamp that hung above him from the ceiling.

"Well, you can tell me more about it later," the man said, speaking from the doorway's threshold, just out of sight. "You rest up. We should be able to move you to a proper bed in a day or two. I'll be back with some water from the well."

Badcock closed his eyes, listening to the man's footsteps echoing down the hallway and then a door creak open. Without realizing it, he fell again into sleep, despite the rays of sunlight covering his face.

A few days passed before Doc Loveless relocated Badcock to a guest bedroom upstairs in his home. The doctor's surgery was in the same house where the doctor lived and saw all of his patients. Doc Loveless had told Badcock he was the only medical doctor anywhere near Tabletop; the next closest doctor was hours away by carriage.

A nightshirt over his freshly changed dressing, Badcock sat up in bed and hungrily ate his lunch of watery oatmeal. He was beginning to gain some of his strength back after the ordeal on the road outside of town, even though he could barely eat because of his stomach wound.

Knocking behind the partially open door, Doc Loveless asked pleasantly, "Can I come in, Benjamin?"

The bright sun pouring in through the bedroom window made Badcock shield his eyes with a hand before answering. "Yes, please do." Badcock put aside the bowl and its porcelain serving tray as Doc Loveless walked to the foot of the brass-railed bed, his black doctor's bag in hand.

"What's my prognosis, Doc?" Badcock asked intently. "It looks like I'm going to live, but how long until I'm healed up?" Badcock didn't think he was in danger but he had no idea where he was. He had never heard of a Doctor Mortimer Loveless of Tabletop before and now feared the town marshal might be looking for him.

"Mortimer, please," Doc Loveless replied casually without answering the question, looking into his bag as he did. "I'm on a first-name basis with all my patients. I've attended to many men like you who've come through Tabletop."

Doc Loveless produced a strange device, a kind of wooden cylinder with a hole bored into either end. He adjusted his bifocal lenses and then tilted his head, putting one end of the device to his ear.

"Is that some kind of wood seashell, Doc? I mean, Mortimer," inquired Badcock mirthfully. "I don't think you'll be able to hear the ocean from where we're at. We're land-locked."

"No, Benjamin," Doc Loveless said calmly, "it's a relatively new medical aid. Now, please open your nightshirt. I'm going to check your heartbeat for any irregularities."

Badcock opened his shirt without further comment and let Doc Loveless listen to his heart beating while he breathed steadily. After a few minutes, Doc Loveless put away the mahogany cylinder, seeming to be satisfied.

37

"You're very fortunate, Benjamin," Doc Loveless pronounced. "Old Clem's bullet nearly went clean through without major damage to the intestines. I believe the risk of infection to be low as of this time."

Doc Loveless adjusted his glasses again as he gazed upward, a mannerism of his associated with moments of reflection. "We only need to keep sanitizing the wound regularly until it's fully healed. I'll remove the sutures I put in then."

"But how long?" asked Badcock again. "I mean, I'm grateful for you putting me up, even saving my life, but I've got people to meet and a business to run."

Doc Loveless cleared his throat. "A month, perhaps longer," he answered, looking at a calendar on the guest bedroom wall. "Bullet wounds to the stomach are among the most egregious injuries. You could have very well died out on that road if I hadn't been riding into town that night."

Badcock grimaced as he heard the news. "What about Old Clem, if that was the man's name?" he asked, feeling slightly dazed. "I killed a man... something I have never done before, so help me. But I swear it was in self-defense."

"That's what it appeared to me," Doc Loveless said. "No one will give a thought about Old Clem or go looking for him. The good people of Tabletop knew he was a drunkard and a troublemaker. But he seemed to think you had wronged him somehow. Did you?"

Badcock replied, "He was a customer, like you said, from earlier that day. He bought a bottle of my bitters and it didn't sit right with him. It's strong stuff, a 'cure-all tonic,' as I say in my pitch to the crowds."

"What's the tonic made from, Benjamin?" asked Doc Loveless inquisitively, seeming to be more than mildly curious. "Could Clem really have been badly sick because of your tonic?"

"I doubt it," Badcock answered hesitantly, unsure himself. "But like I said, it's strong medicine, and the cure can sometimes be worse than the ailment."

Looking around nervously as if confused, Badcock asked, "Where's my wagon, anyhow? My goods and inventory, are they safe? That's my entire livelihood in that wagon."

"Your wagon is safe," Doc Loveless assured him. "I was able to unstick your wheel and get the wagon out of the road. It's secured behind this residence right now."

Badcock exhaled but said nothing, not entirely certain his goods were fine even after the doctor's explanation.

"Alright then," Doc Loveless said, ending the conversation with a pat on Badcock's shoulder. "I'll leave you to rest. And let me take that tray for you. Dinner will be after six o'clock this evening. Yet more oatmeal, I'm afraid."

The evening came soon, the sun slowly setting outside Badcock's window, leaving the room dark except for the moonlight on its windowsill. Badcock hadn't left the house since his arrival; he'd been using a basin supplied and emptied daily by Doc Loveless to relieve himself instead of venturing to the outhouse. He could barely walk in his condition as it was.

Where's dinner? thought Badcock urgently, wishing Loveless would at least come in to turn on the gas lamp on the room's dresser. Badcock suddenly realized that he had neither seen nor heard anyone else in the house except for Doc Loveless; the good doctor had yet to mention a wife and children or even other patients. Were there any?

Hours passed, the moon clouded over, and the waning moonlight outside the window created an eerie shadow world within the spacious bedroom. Badcock knew he could walk if needed as he had made it up the stairs to the house's second floor, albeit with Doc Loveless' assistance. He wondered if he should look for the absent doctor or stay in bed.

A sudden creaking noise caught his ear as soft footsteps trod over the floorboards somewhere beyond his bedroom. Doc Loveless had left Badcock's bedroom door cracked slightly open, and he could see there was no light coming from the hallway.

"Doc? I mean, Mortimer?" Badcock called out from his seat on the bed, his voice growing louder as if to insulate himself from any danger. "Are you there?"

A light blinked on from somewhere in the hall, but there came no reply, only the groan of a door opening. Badcock winced as he pulled himself to the edge of the bed, letting his legs flop limply over the side of the mattress. He then stood with some effort, the wound in his gut reminding him that he might not get very far from where he had lain.

Walking stiffly to the door, Badcock grasped its knob and steadied himself, eventually stepping out into the dark hallway. The light he had seen was coming from another room—one at the hall's opposite end. The door to the room was ajar as if beckoning him to enter.

Slowly, he reached the door's threshold and peered in. A bearded man in a black suit sat at a writing desk, the light emanating from a gas lamp at its corner. His expression was pained, and he seemed engrossed in thought as he wrote fixedly with a quilled ink pen.

Badcock then recognized the man: it was his first business partner, Arthur Comstock. Badcock had swindled Arthur of much of their shared funds and then left town, leaving him to likely face bankruptcy. Soon after, Badcock had formulated his tonic bitters using the money he had gained by cheating Arthur. Badcock had never found out what became of him.

Comstock put down his pen and wept softly, his face cradled in the palms of his hands. He opened the desk drawer and took out a small pistol. Fatigued and defeated, he stared at the gun for a moment and then stood, fading into the shadows as the room went black.

Leaning on the door's frame, Badcock turned as he heard a rope being hoisted somewhere in the house, its supporting wood creaking in response. He left the room and stood at the top of the stairs. Below him, at the bottom of the stairs, the figure of a man kneeled, a soft white glow surrounding him in the darkness.

Straining, Badcock kept a hand pressed against the walls of the staircase as he descended to the floor below. The kneeling man was Atsa, his Indian guide in the territories, who he had betrayed for a bounty and then fled. Atsa's hands were tied behind his back, his long hair draped across his face.

Atsa staggered as he was yanked to his feet by some force, then ascended nearby gallows steps, an empty noose waiting for him. The white glow illuminating the scene dimmed and went dark as the rope was placed around Atsa's neck, a tear running down his cheek.

Feeling ill, Badcock wiped beads of sweat from his forehead. A sickening dread washed over him as he grabbed the stairs' railing, weak and frightened. Where was he really? Was all this a nightmare brought on by some infection-induced fever?

A light came on in the house's kitchen, not far from the stairs. Badcock heard someone rummaging through cabinets and a child quietly weeping, her terrible sorrow palpable even from where he was taking his short reprieve.

Pushing himself forward, Badcock stopped in the doorway of the kitchen. A haggard woman was desperately searching the place as if looking for something to eat, but she found only bare cupboards. A small girl wearing a tattered dress sat on the floor, crying, her face hollow and emaciated.

It was his wife, Patience, and his young daughter, Charity. After *The Medicine Show* had begun to make profits, he had decided to abandon them, no longer wanting to provide for a family while on the road for so many months at a time. Patience had no way of supporting herself and Charity, so Badcock supposed they had fallen into poverty and perhaps even starved to death.

The kitchen darkened, leaving only Doc Loveless waiting at the end of the hall, his expressionless face revealed by the light spilling from the adjoining dining room.

"Doc, what's going on here?" Badcock said, his voice quiet, almost timid now. "Why am I seeing these things?"

"These scenes are the legacy of your life, Benjamin," Doc Loveless replied as an unsettling silence descended over them. "This is what you have left behind in the world past."

"World past?" Badcock almost fell into shock as he heard this. "Am I dead, Doc? But shouldn't I be in Heaven then?"

"Why would you be, Benjamin?" Doc Loveless seemed almost amused, his lips slowly curling into a sinister smile.

"Because my business is helping people, Doc," Badcock interjected, a rising hysteria in his tone. "It's been my life's work. I sell hope to the hopeless and dreams to the dreamless. People need what I give them. I'm the good Samaritan."

Saying nothing in reply, Doc Loveless instead gestured toward Badcock with an open hand before motioning toward the dining room. "Come, you're the guest of honor at this gathering. There are still others you must meet tonight."

Badcock clutched the hallway's walls with each step, holding himself up until he reached the dining room's doorway. Doc Loveless slipped out of view as Badcock entered the dining room. Guests were gathered around a long table decked with china plates and domed silver cloches, at which were set high-backed chairs.

"Sit here," Doc Loveless bid Badcock, his hand indicating the unoccupied chair at the head of the dining table. "Dinner is served."

Instead of sitting, Badcock stood at the head of the table and looked out at the guests. Comstock was seated nearby, dark, treacly blood oozing from a gaping hole in his temple. Atsa sat across from him, his head tilted to one side, his swollen neck broken. Patience sat next to Atsa, her skin ashen and eyes sunken, resembling a smiling skeleton.

Other guests were seated along the table, their faces showing signs of terrible maladies and terminal diseases brought upon them with the aid of Badcock's "cure-all" tonic. The macabre guests watched Badcock intently as if waiting for him to take his seat and begin the meal.

Badcock gazed down at his dinner. A silver cloche covered his plate, just like the others. He cautiously removed the cloche and saw the head of a young girl: his daughter Charity's, its skin blotted by pestilence, its eyes closed shut.

The head's eyelids snapped open as Badcock put the cloche next to the plate. Its blackened tongue lolled out of its mouth, its eyes rolling back into their sockets as the head produced a putrid gurgling noise. The dinner guests lifted the cloches from their plates, unveiling piles of bloody, cancerous tumors as the main course. Badcock then saw his gut had become a mass of squirming maggots, teeming and festering in the place he'd been shot.

Doc Loveless' eyes were pitch black as he spoke, his voice hollow as if he was speaking from a distance void. "You've always served me, Benjamin Badcock, even without you being aware of it. But now, you will be the guest of honor for an endless night of ghoulish feasts set before you on gilded platters for all eternity."

Badcock screamed but there was no one to hear him. His place at the table would always be there, and the spectral dinner guests would always be waiting for him, his banquet companions, until the end of time.

The man in the cattle hat leaned over the fatally wounded Badcock as he took his last dying breaths, his hands resting over his knees. Badcock's vision seemed to focus for a moment, but then his head slumped to its side, his eyes closing for good with a faint gasp.

"See, I was right," the cattleman told his compadre, who was still on horseback. "Two gunshots back from wheres I came; I knew he was in some trouble. But I reckon we're too late to help him."

The man on the horse asked, "Should we fetch the town marshal then? It's not like we can hide this here wagon nowheres. Someone might come lookin'."

"No, I doubts it," the cattleman said with a pleased smirk. "It's nighttime and I'd wager no one heard the shots 'cept us. Let's jus' take what bills is in that paper box in the wagon and we'll be on our way. Make it look like a robbery, which it might have been anyway. Ain't no one gonna miss ol' Benjamin Badcock."

The Boneless King

T he door was unlocked, which Wes hadn't expected. Un-
needed for the moment, he put the spare key back
into the pocket of his jeans for safekeeping. He opened the
cabin's peeling, weather-beaten entryway, revealing a musty,
neglected interior.

A single square room made up the entire space within.
Thick curtains had been pulled over the cabin's handful of
grimy windows and soft light spilled through several thread-
bare spots, illuminating the otherwise darkish place.

Wes strode to the room's center, dropping his canvas duffel
bag onto the creaking floor. He hastily looked about as if
searching for something. There wasn't much furniture, only
a four-legged wooden table, a solitary wood chair to go with
it, and a battered couch resting in front of the empty stone
fireplace.

He must have used the couch to sleep, Wes thought, spying
a rolled wool blanket and two pillows. A thin layer of dust
coated the silent room, likely proof that his missing uncle
hadn't been back to this remote refuge in recent months.

But there was this: a reel-to-reel tape recorder sitting on
the flat wood table with a short stack of notebooks piled
haphazardly nearby. The tape recorder was large and shaped
like a box. The reels contained a full spool of tape, enough
to capture hours of audio. A small, hand-held microphone
was attached to the recorder, its slim cord loose.

Wes hovered above the table's well-worn chair, gingerly brushing away some grime with a hand before taking a seat. The tape recorder was plugged into a wall outlet, its power cable hanging over the table's edge. He turned the dial to *PLAY*. He listened as the reels began to slowly turn, a faint crackling noise soon quelled by the smooth, authoritative voice of the cabin's owner, Uncle Gordon.

I've returned from my year-long sojourn among the Munggua *people. This formerly uncontacted tribe has endured as part of a fascinating, nearly pre-Neolithic culture found only on the island's western portion. Their numbers are few, but the* Munggua *have held out in the unexplored jungles for many, many generations, perhaps since the earliest human habitation.*

Within such an expansive area, the Munggua *persisted in isolation until these past few years, making their ways unknown to outsiders. The* Munggua *even seemed to have believed they were the only people in existence, occupying a world all their own. My command of the native languages of these islands and my offering of gifts allowed me to live with these people and learn some of their most closely held secrets.*

Turning the recorder's dial to *STOP*, Wes began sorting through the piled notebooks on the table. Their pages were torn in places and sometimes heavily stained, as if Uncle Gordon had been writing while out in the field as he observed the practices of the *Munggua*. He randomly opened one of the notebooks and began to read a cursive, hand-written entry:

The necessary extract for the ritual is derived from several indigenous plants found in the jungles surrounding our village. Each inflorescent plant is poisonous in a large enough dose but, when measured and then mixed, the effect is that of a neuroleptic instead.

The subject of the ritual must consume this substance from the shaman guide's bowl approximately one hour before its commence-

ment. Otherwise, the shock will kill the subject before the final transformation is accomplished.

Wes closed the laboratory-style notebook and examined its cover. A date range was jotted on adhesive tape near the cover's top, but nothing indicated its contents.

There were ten notebooks, each detailing about a month's worth of entries. Wes decided it would be easier to listen to the tape recordings and then peruse the notebooks later. Perhaps his uncle had left some clue about his current whereabouts near the end of his tapes. Wes' first year of medical school was over, and he now had a several-month break to delve into this mystery.

The sun shone brightly as Wes stood on the cabin's threshold and scrutinized the limber pine woods around him, the midday light sharply contrasting with the murky gloom within the cabin's four walls. He lit a cigarette and walked along the dirt trail leading up from the narrow combe where the cabin was nestled to a ridge above the valley.

Wes had hiked miles from the tertiary road where he had parked his rented truck to reach this spot. The forested valley was so secluded that no other homes were anywhere near it, the cabin idling in complete solitude. The previous owners had built the rustic abode as a hunting lodge of sorts.

Only he and Uncle Gordon knew about this place; Wes' father (Uncle Gordon's brother) was unaware it even existed. Before leaving on this last sabbatical to the islands, his uncle had bought the small property for cash. He had visited only once, living far away otherwise. Along with its deed, Uncle Gordon had included simple directions to the cabin, hiding both documents in a steel box in Wes' basement.

Why the secrecy? Uncle Gordon had told Wes he was the only one he could trust with the box. He'd hoped that Wes would take over his studies one day, delving into the mysteries of the world's primitive peoples. He also seemed to hint that something important might be left for Wes at the cabin someday. What Uncle Gordon had intended to accomplish with this place was still unclear, its purpose elusive to his nephew. But he wanted to keep the secret.

Wes looked out over a panorama of hills and valleys as he stood atop the ridge, stark white snow still cresting distant summits even in the early summer. He finished his cigarette and tossed the butt onto the ground, taking a deep breath of the cool mountain air. Wes remembered when his uncle had first disappeared, near the end of that exploratory field leave he'd taken from his research position, and how Wes' father, Craig, had done his best to help the police and Uncle Gordon's university with the open investigation.

"We've looked everywhere in this apartment," Craig said as he put another manila folder on the kitchen table, adding to the stack already there. "The police came up empty-handed, so we're wasting our time. I fear Gordon may really be the victim of foul play."

Craig seemed pained and then continued after a sigh of tired exasperation. "My brother maintained fastidious records of his personal affairs, Wes. There's nothing Gordon might have kept here that Detective Becker could use in a missing persons case. We just have Gordon's financial papers, some legal documents, and..."

"What's this?" Wes interrupted, having opened the last folder taken from Uncle Gordon's home office by Craig. He then held up a medical form filled out with a typewriter. "This looks like a recent diagnosis from Uncle Gordon's physician," Wes clarified, now seemingly intrigued. "But I'm not sure what it's about."

"Please let me see it," Craig requested, now standing over Wes, who was seated on a kitchen chair. His father quickly skimmed the form and then turned it over to read its back. "Hmmm," Craig murmured, scratching his temple for a moment. "I found this folder under some loose papers at the bottom of a desk drawer. The police must've missed this.

"It's a diagnosis for malignant glioma, a cancerous brain tumor," he finally announced, surprised. "And this is from a neurologist, not Gordon's regular doctor. There's also a recommendation for treatment and surgery following the diagnosis."

"Then Uncle Gordon could have been dying?" Wes asked urgently, realizing they may have found a genuine clue as to what had happened to his uncle.

"Yes, almost certainly," replied Craig as he read back over the form in his hands. "Even with the tumor's removal, the survival rate for glioblastoma is low. Gordon had a few more years at most. I'll have to show this to Detective Becker tomorrow."

Wes paused, uneasy, before asking another question. "He may have taken his own life instead of wasting away from cancer." Wes doubted this even as he said it; Uncle Gordon was a stalwart fighter if ever there was one. He would have never resignedly accepted his death from a disease. The man loved life more than anyone Wes had ever known.

"He could have, but where's the body? Something should have been found by now," Craig offered in response. "The passenger manifest recorded that he was on his return flight, but there's no trace of him after that. It's as if he vanished into thin air without so much as a parting goodbye."

"There's also no record here of a follow-up with the neurologist after his initial diagnosis," Wes indicated as he closed Uncle Gordon's medical records, putting the folder with its remaining papers on the stack. "He just left for his sabbatical without any further treatment, it seems. Odd that he wouldn't have tried to buy more time with surgery."

"True," Craig agreed, his voice becoming quiet; he seemed to be holding something back from Wes. "But, if he just wanted to die alone, why would he come back home? He didn't see any of us after his return. If he was planning an anonymous suicide, why not do it out on that faraway island, where no one would ever find the body?"

Wes rested at the table with the tape recorder, deciding not to smoke while in the cabin. He was worried cigarette smoke might somehow damage his uncle's tapes, and the air in the cabin was already quite noisome without tobacco fumes being added in.

Uncle Gordon had been very much alive after his plane trip home, Wes thought. He had returned to this cabin and chronicled his stay among the *Munggua* for some archival purpose. But how had Uncle Gordon arrived here (Wes hadn't seen a vehicle beside the only accessible road for many miles) and what had happened after these tapes were recorded?

He pressed *PLAY* again and the tape reels turned, Uncle Gordon's voice assuming a relaxed, narrational tone:

I have spent considerable time in other parts of this archipelago. However, the magnificent vastness of the western island's lush trop-ical boscage still takes my breath away. When viewed from the high hills not far from my hosts' village, the jungle canopy seems to have no end. The Munggua *people live in a kind of untouched paradise, bountiful, where everything they could desire is within their reach. Even post-contact, the* Munggua *remain fiercely protective of their privacy and native autonomy.*

Their connection to the land is a profound one and informs their spiritual views. Reality to them is the flowering sago tree; the blue ocean; a turbulent, unchecked river; and the almost immeasurable, trackless mangrove swamp—these were the whole universe to the Munggua *until strangers intruded upon their way of life.*

The Munggua *believe that spirits inhabit all things, even their bodily extremities. Certain spirits live in a man's fingers or nose, for example, and can cause mischief if offended or otherwise provoked. The* Munggua *also contend the spirits of their ancestors live on and watch over them, granting immense power that can be possessed through intricate ceremony and ritual sacrifice.*

Herein lies my interest in these fervent, often pitiless people: tribes I encountered on the island farther south during previous expedi-

tions relayed tales of folk who could metamorphize a man into a giant worm, the resultant worm form attaining nigh-immortality, even near godhood.

The name of this ritual of metamorphosis can be translated as "the Boneless King," referring to the worm's status as an invertebrate. It was this tribe's most sacred rite, and they considered it proof of their mastery over nature and the spiritual world.

The tribesmen who related this fable to me insisted it was true despite the apparently fantastical elements. They then said the tribe who practiced this rite lived on the same island and were reputed to be flesh eaters. The tribe was greatly feared and its members were left to themselves, having headhunted their neighbors to extinction in the distant past.

When the Munggua were first discovered by Westerners, the description of their territory and the peoples' characteristics matched that of the "Boneless King" tales told to me by the island's local tribes. Given my condition, I knew that I must seek out the Munggua and learn the secret of their ritual. I had a rapport with the island people and there was nothing left for me other than to pursue this chance to cheat death.

Uncle Gordon's narrative was cut short as Wes again put the recorder's dial to *STOP*. He rummaged through his duffel bag, which he had left near the cabin's tiny kitchenette, and finally removed a large brown envelope.

Wes slid from the envelope a black and white photograph, examining it closely. The photo was of Dr. Gordon Klingler, taken some years ago during his first journey to the islands.

Square-jawed and confident, Uncle Gordon stood at the center of a cluster of natives grasping spears. The men were grim-faced, as if enduring some unwanted intrusion. Uncle Gordon appeared oblivious to the men's demeanor, smiling broadly at the camera in his jungle attire, his shirt sleeves rolled up to his forearms.

Putting the photo back, Wes searched the cabinets above the kitchenette's sink. He found two cans of corned beef hash and opened them with an opener he found next to them. *Uncle Gordon didn't leave much food*, Wes thought, disappointed. *I'm glad I brought some of my own.*

One of the electric stove's burners glowed orange, a covered steel pot resting atop it. Wes drank thirstily from the sink faucet, hands cupped as there were no drinking glasses. The rusted, iron-mineral taste of the well water was disagreeable. He could faintly detect the whirring of a generator, the sound coming from somewhere below the cabin's floorboards.

He also left the generator running—a fire hazard, Wes considered, mildly concerned. *He must have, or I wouldn't have been able to run the tapes or use the stove. I wonder how much fuel I have left? I'll have to check later.*

Wes spooned the warmed hash onto a plate and went outside for lunch. He sat on some level rocks piled next to a thicket of trees and ate his simple meal in the afternoon sun. The old generator's whirring could be heard from outside as he was sitting close to the cabin; he heard it intermittently falter with a sputter.

Heading back inside, Wes pressed *PLAY* again and sat at the table. Uncle Gordon's voice now sounded vaguely anxious.

So, for months, I lived with the Munggua. *They shared their rich oral tradition with me, celebrating and venerating their ancestors, who they believe are still with them. As the* Munggua *and related island people have no written language, all their collective science, religion, history, and cosmology is passed on through storytelling, generation after generation.*

I've transcribed much of their language in my notebooks, finding it very similar to many native dialects on the islands but with some remarkable distinctions. After some months, I felt I had gained these people's confidence. The Munggua *seemed to see in me a kindred soul despite my outsider's appearance.*

Then, one night, the Munggua *head man—his name is Kolokam—told me a new story, one I hadn't heard from any other villagers before or subsequently. This story may be the tribe's oldest and, while not exactly a creation myth, it certainly includes the origin of the* Munggua *as a people.*

In this story, a man called Gimi wanders alone for what seems like an eternity, moving from place to place, until he comes upon an uninhabited forest that will one day become the heart of the Munggua's *tribal lands. Spent from his long travels, he falls to the ground under the sprawling jungle's tightly entwined cover, sinking into a deep and interminable sleep.*

Around Gimi's head, limbs, and bodily trunk, the tangled under-brush's porous soil begins to claim him as he slumbers, restful and unaware. He is drawn down into the soupy, terrestrial detritus of the jungle floor, changing and reforming into a colossal, man-sized worm within this thin layer of earth.

More people come to this place and, eventually, Gimi becomes their king and is worshipped by them as a deity of the forest and the land. He protects his people and watches over them, elevating worthy elders to become "Boneless Kings," a kind of sainthood among the Munggua. *In the ground under their sacred place, these ancestors are ensconced, dormant in prolonged estivation but still heedful and aware.*

This is the legend! This is why I came to the Munggua; *so that I could learn this ritual of "the Boneless King," apparently as real as I had hoped.*

I questioned Kolokam, asking if he had ever seen an elder trans-formed into one of the revered guardian worms. Reluctant at first, he then said that he had and that it had been an incredible sight to behold.

I asked if I could witness the ritual and whether an elder had been chosen or soon would be. Kolokam was silent. He then slowly said one had been chosen and that he would be the spirit guide to lead the transformation.

The Munggua *had intended that I would leave them before the ritual, but Kolokam told me I could view it if I so desired. The ritual would be held on the night of the new moon, in the thick of the jungle outside the village.*

The night of the new moon came. I was led to a secluded spot, perhaps a mile from where the Munggua *maintained their settlement of thatched huts and flimsy rattan enclosures. A village man said they had kept this place in the jungle hidden from me until they felt I could be fully trusted. Now, I was to see their most secretive and closely held rite take place.*

I stood at the edge of a jungle clearing, perhaps with as many as a dozen other men within view. Upright wooden poles carved with the symbols of headhunting adorned the clearing's edges. From the poles hung shrunken human heads, the mouths of these unfortunates stitched tightly shut.

Standing torches were interspersed among the headhunting poles, their burning fires illuminating a bed of turned-up soil at the clearing's center. A naked man, very elderly and wizened, was guided by each arm and then lain down in the soil. The man appeared quite groggy and benumbed, as if he was thoroughly intoxicated.

The old man placed his arms over his chest and closed his eyes. Kolokam appeared from the jungle's inky shadows, festooned in a bird-feathered shaman's headdress and chalk-white face paint. A bone ornament fashioned from the tusks of a wild boar protruded from his nose and his expression was contorted into an unnerving grin.

Kolokam was now as fearsome as could be imagined. He let out a savage howl as he stood above the supine elder. His ceremonial stave was held aloft, its raw wood twisted into the shape of a writhing flatworm.

The other men from the village drummed and sang and danced, Kolokam chanting a refrain as they shrieked and ululated. They leaped from one side of the clearing to the other and gyrated frantically, a coarse sweat drenching their nearly bare bodies.

With their mouths hanging open, the men's eyes lolled back in their heads, the spirits of this dark place having seized them and taken possession of their souls. I felt as if I was peering through a window into the distant past, glimpsing a primeval spectacle that might have been found at the dawn of man's antiquity.

As this enthralling display progressed, the elder suddenly began to stir, his body at first showing only a tremor but then falling into spastic convulsions. A man, a prisoner, was brought forth and tied to one of the headhunting poles. Kolokam would later tell me that the man had murdered his brother and that this was his punishment: to be consumed in an act of sacrificial cannibalism.

The elder's body bulged horrifically, his skin taking on a slick, jet-black sheen. His limbs and torso swelled enormously before collapsing into the shape of a monstrous dark brown worm, the pointed head long and snout-like.

The worm slithered toward the man lashed to the pole. The man tried to scream but his tongue had been cut out. His eyes protruded in terror as the worm engulfed his lower half, a glistening secretion beginning to dissolve his appendages.

I was both fascinated and repulsed by what was happening. The man soon went limp, the remainder of his carcass eventually disappearing into the smothering folds of the giant worm. Satiated, the worm burrowed into the soil where only moments before its human form had commenced the ritual, taking its place in the earth among the Munggua's *forefathers.*

The sun had almost set, and the cabin was dimly lit from the outside. Wes put the recorder's dial to *STOP* when he finally noticed that evening had come. The jarring tale on Uncle Gordon's tapes had made him forget where he was and what was around him.

A single light bulb dangled from the cabin's panel ceiling, unshielded and unlit. Wes stood to pull the lightbulb's cord and bright light filled the cabin's middle interior, leaving the table and chair where he had sat still in shadows.

Wes took a cigarette from a pack in his duffel bag and opened the cabin's front door. The air outside was cool, but the evening was warmer than the last. Soon, these mountains would bask in the summer heat, as they always did.

Lighting his cigarette, Wes inhaled its flavor, taking in a long draw through the cigarette's filter. He stared into the cabin from where he sat on a tree stump, the door propped open, light from the cabin ceiling's lightbulb spilling out into the surrounding night.

Wes recalled that, when his father had dropped him off at home after searching Uncle Gordon's off-campus apartment, he had told Wes something odd, even disturbing. Wes supposed it might have come from the apprehension that Wes had sensed in his father when they'd discussed Uncle Gordon's speculative murder or suicide.

Its wide bumper coming close to the sidewalk facing Wes' modest one-story bungalow, Craig parked his convertible, Wes beside him in the passenger seat. Craig hoped Wes would be able to afford something better after medical school—that he might even purchase his first home if he wed after graduating. But Wes was still single as far as he knew; he was tight-lipped about girls, as always.

"Well, here we are," Craig announced, watching his son push open the car door from the front seat. "I'll tell you what Detective Becker says after we speak on Monday."

Wes paused on the edge of his car seat and turned to look at his father. "Do you really think your brother would take his own life?" Wes asked emphatically, raising his voice. "That would be so unlike Uncle Gordon. I can't believe he'd ever do it."

"Neither do I, really," Craig replied, looking away from Wes onto the empty street, his expression preoccupied. "That's why I first suggested he was murdered. Years ago, Gordon confided something to me that I still think about."

"Like he was going to disappear someday? Something like that?" Wes tensed, silently pleading with his father to not share something even worse.

"No," Craig answered. *"He said that he would find a way to live forever, that he'd discover the secret of eternal life. Really. Gordon was entirely serious. He said this after his maiden voyage to the islands, quite a few years ago. Seems very strange now, especially after his disappearance. I don't know what to make of it."*

Closing the cabin door behind him, Wes sat on the table's chair and pressed *PLAY*. Uncle Gordon resumed his account of the *Munggua* and their customs.

There have been small signs of my growing weakness since I've been on the island. Dizziness, as well as some nausea—I even almost vomited once or twice. I haven't let Kolokam or the rest of the Munggua *know that I am dying. If I did, they likely would have never allowed me to participate in the ritual, even as a trusted observer. My reasons for wanting to see the rite of "the Boneless King" would have been all too transparent.*

In bits and pieces, Kolokam revealed to me just what is in the neuroleptic extract used in the ritual. I've recorded this information in my field notes. Interestingly, Kolokam stated that all that's necessary for the transformation is the botanical extract and the soil of the sacred grove, so infused with mystical potency is the earth there from millennia of ancestor worms resting under the dirt. The ritual chanting and cavorting are entirely for show, done to reaffirm the Munggua*'s religious traditions.*

And a sacrifice. The sacrifice of a prisoner is effective, but the ritual's success is almost guaranteed if a close family member is used in a prisoner's place. That the chosen relation voluntarily comes to the place of sacrifice is an absolute requirement.

The worm form can be achieved with only the first two components of the ritual. Still, the new worm can only become forever undying with the sacrifice of a human life. A life for a life eternal.

I plan on digging in the sacred grove late at night while the village sleeps, obtaining enough soil to...

Without warning, the light went out in the cabin and the tape recording stopped as if the power had been abruptly cut off. Surprised, Wes stumbled from his seat and groped his way to his duffel bag, finding the camping flashlight he had brought for the trip. He flipped the flashlight's top switch on and a wide beam shone onto the cabin floor, allowing him to see again.

I need to find the trapdoor to the cellar; it's got to be in a corner somewhere, Wes reasoned, probing around the room with his light. *The generator's down there. Maybe it finally ran out of fuel.*

A dusty floor mat was in a corner past the couch where Uncle Gordon had set up his improvised bed. Wes turned over the mat with a foot, exposing a trapdoor with a handle. The hatch didn't seem to be locked.

Resting the flashlight on top of the tarp mat's turned-up leaf, Wes grabbed the hatch's iron ring and pulled, opening the trapdoor onto a set of short wooden stairs. Flashlight in hand, Wes crept down the steps into the darkness below.

The earthen cellar smelled of wet soil and gasoline, its underground atmosphere likely as stale as the cabin's air when he had arrived this morning. Crouching slightly beneath the low ceiling, Wes shined his flashlight along the cellar's walls, spying the idle generator near its back. He began to step forward in search of any fuel canisters he might use.

The ground beneath him was spongy as he approached, gleaming under the beam of his flashlight, seemingly saturated with a fine coating of slime. His foot then sank, involuntarily caught on something.

A glinting, pointed tail whipped from the moistened dirt, wrapping itself around Wes' legs and contorting around his waist and belly. He gasped in utter panic, falling back only to be enveloped by the humongous worm's fleshy interior lobes, digestive fluids dousing him.

One of Wes' arms was pulled into the worm's spiraling folds, corrosive mucus burning his skin. Wes cried out and struggled feebly, his remaining arm quickly consumed and then finally his head, overwhelmed by the turning and undulating of the worm's massive body.

The invertebrate worm form of Uncle Gordon lay in the hallowed soil of the *Munggua*, having achieved its primordial deification. It once again submerged itself in the earthen cellar floor, lying in wait for the warmer days ahead.

A Hunger So...

I am the sole survivor of an unfortunate shipwreck, having been plunged into an unforgiving ocean during a raging storm. I was saved from certain death only by the Whim of Fate or, perhaps, an Angel of Christ's Mercy. The faithful captain of our doomed vessel—may God rest his soul—and our steadfast crew only witnessed the menacing storm clouds and churning waves on the late evening horizon when it had become too late.

The storm fell upon us almost without warning, a sudden downpour followed by a punishing deluge. All were swept from the ship's deck, sending us tumbling into the eye of the tempest. That I quickly clung to some floating debris while others were pulled down into a watery grave is entirely a matter of Divine Providence and can only be explained by the Will of Our Lord.

After that dreadful night, I lay on a deserted beach, the tides having brought me in under cover of darkness. Amongst the briny froth I fell into unconsciousness but then awoke to the morning sun, a reminder that I yet lived.

The unknown island's white sands reflected brightly under my shoe-buckled feet, the cloudless sky a hue of pure azure blue. Palm trees swayed in the halcyon breeze not far from where I walked, acting as guardians to the island's lush interior. But what seemed to me like a veritable Paradise would only become a special Hell, as I'll soon relate.

I stood among the pulpy detritus left along the shoreline by our former ship, *The Ascension*, picking through the shattered wood and torn sailcloth, searching for anything I could use to survive. I found a broken mast, still intact enough to be of service.

I dragged the damaged mast fixedly over the beach's sands with a plan to construct a shelter against some rocks that faced the ocean. I decided to not chance venturing beneath the island's tropical canopy until I was more certain of any dangers that may be present, fearing I could not be alone here on what seemed a deserted island in uncharted seas.

The mid-morning sun was quite strong, yet the air was still pleasantly mild due to the wafting breeze from the ocean. I worked feverishly, sweat beading my brow, not wanting to be caught unshielded when the sun rose even higher. Nonetheless, I was thankful for the sun's brightness, for it allowed me to clearly see the task at hand.

I fashioned the mast's wood into a sturdy frame for my provisional shelter, the constituent parts having come apart with some effort. Gathering heavy fern leaves from the jungle's periphery, I securely thatched an improvised roof for my new home, ruefully anticipating yet another violent storm off the ocean waters.

My labor had been quick and efficient, absolute desperation driving me to toil as fast as possible. After several hours, my domicile was complete, the rays of the equatorial sun at its zenith no longer a threat. I collapsed under the beach hut's merciful shade and surveyed my efforts; I had done well. Better than I had anticipated.

I took in all that surrounded me from my resting spot: surging cerulean swells capped with white foam crashing over barren sea stacks; scattered flocks of squawking seagulls flitting through the air; the unfamiliar ocean that seemed to extend out forever from these lonely, nameless shores, taunting me as the only means of escape from my archipelago prison.

This distant island was likely not found on any map. What would become of me? Was rescue something I could truly hope for, even with the Good Grace of my Savior? I now had nothing more than hope and the will to survive.

I pushed my perturbations aside as I needed both fresh water and comestible sustenance, my parched throat and empty stomach no longer tolerable. Potable water could be found only by exploring more of the island, the proximate ocean's salty brine offering nothing upon which to live except the chance of some fish.

Scaling a nearby hillock, I stood and looked out over the verdant swathe of tropical forest beyond the beach's shores. The island was so large I couldn't view its entirely from my perch; the hillock may not have been of the proper elevation, perhaps. More white-sand beaches framed the island's coastline to the west and east, but I knew I wouldn't be able to discern the island's northern end without the aid of a spyglass, if at all.

I then caught sight of what I thought might be a pool of water amongst the dense vegetation, sunlight reflecting from it, less than a league from my observation spot. Feeling faint from dehydration, I hurried down into the jungle, striving to maintain a straight line to my goal as I strode through the snarled underbrush.

Near exhaustion and beaten by the sun, I came to a crystalline waterfall pouring over a cliff into its pristine basin. At last! I would have fresh water! I wasted no time.

Doffing my shoes and peeling my ragged shirt and breeches from me, I stumbled into the pool, took a few steps, and then fell face forward with a splash. My sunburnt skin was soothed as if with a wondrous balm, and I took a mouthful with both hands cupped, my long-suffering throat finally receiving a welcome reprieve.

The basin was not very deep, and I could clearly see to its sandy bottom. Wading back, I squatted in the shallows and drank as much as I could. But my stomach was still unfilled, and I worried as to where I might find food.

Something moved among my clothes near the brush, seen from the corner of my eye. What was it? A small animal, black furred. It disappeared into the jungle as soon as I leveled my gaze to where the thing had been.

Dressing, I surveyed my surroundings and saw no creature. What could it have been? From what I knew of these islands' flora and fauna, few pileous beasts made their home here, most animal life being fish or feathered birds.

There must be fruits, I thought. I needed only to find the plants from which they hung themselves, ripe in bloom. Soon, I found a viridescent fruit growing in abundance in a forest clump not far from the waterfall, its sweet, seed-laden flesh satiating what had become a gnawing pain. The fruits sprouted from their trees' low branches and were easily harvested; I took more with me as I departed.

My ramshackle lean-to on the beach was undisturbed, just as I had left it. I planned how I would gather more food, deciding to search for a different path through the jungle tomorrow. Tonight, I would have to make a fire, else I would sit only in darkness with just the waxing moon over the nighttime waters to keep me company.

As the vivid orange sun began its low drift over the ocean, I scavenged the beach for anything of use. Chunks of wood from my ship's mast had dried under the day's basking sun and were now suitable for kindling. I gathered smooth bone-white stones and laid them in a tight circle, piling wood and then clumps of grass into a heap within the stone circle's boundary.

I kept a piece of flint in a pouch under my belt, one of the few things not lost to me when I had struggled upon the ocean's surface. Some sparks from the flint flew onto the pile as I made use of my primitive tool, lighting a fire that then began to blaze. I sat and stared into the darting flames created by my efforts, the first manifestation of civilization I had seen since washing ashore.

I reclined in the lean-to, the crackling fire close but not enough to pose a hazard, satisfied it would burn for most of the night now that the sun had set. Sleepy, I rested my head on folded hands and lay back on the sand, wishing I had a cushion for comfort.

Again, I saw it, this time through half-closed eyes: the black-furred vermin from the jungle I had witnessed earlier. As my eyes opened fully, I could now clearly see it was a smallish rat, my vision focusing in my campfire's flickering light.

The tiny creature watched me intently and, strangely, as if with purpose. It stood upright on its hind legs, paws pendulous in front of its chest. The rat's whiskers twitched as its bright eyes reflected the nearby flames. It was sure to stay back, out of arm's reach, as if it was aware I might be a danger to it.

Then, without a squeak, the rat scurried off, disappearing into the darkness of the nighttime beach. I looked about for more of them, relieved that my visitor appeared to have been without any fellows. I worried they might come as I slept, but I had some assurance that the burning woodfire would keep the curious rats at bay.

I drifted into sleep with one eye barely open until it too finally closed in exhaustion. Dark, terrifying visions came upon me as I lay in slumber, of gnawing, ravenous maws tearing into me, devouring my weary flesh in bloody morsels. But I awoke as dawn came, whole in body and alone on the beach, with only the morning breeze and the rising sun to greet me.

Surely there must be a nest of these creatures somewhere, I thought to myself as I examined the trunk of a palm tree. Once found, I could smoke them out with a bonfire and remove this threat to my well-being, which was endangering my eventual rescue from the island. I needed to make a torch and then, when lit, set the rat hovel aflame, destroying the miniature devil spawn. Such was my plan.

I dried fibers from the palm tree, torn free with care. I then bundled them around a stout stick from the underbrush and tied them with loose fiber threads until, eventually, I had the implement I'd sought. When needed, I would set the torch ablaze with my flint stone, ready for its purpose.

But where were the rats and their nest? My unlit torch in hand, I returned to the waterfall, a cool respite from the growing heat of the day. As I sat by the pool's sandy bank, I surmised they could be near, as I had first seen the rat here. There had to be others, perhaps many more.

I returned to the fruit grove I had discovered earlier and searched for signs of the rats. Droppings and nibbled, rotted gourds that had fallen from their branchlets were strewn amongst the trees. They came here to feed, likely in numbers.

After selecting a few gourds for myself, I moved some distance away and hid in the brush. I kept a watchful eye on the trees' exposed roots, which rose and arched from the island's rich soil. Some time passed and, as the sun waned, one rat appeared, and then several more. The hungry beasts sought the partially eaten gourds in the shade, where they rested and resumed their feasting.

Once its belly was full, the last rat left, and I stood to watch where the animal went as it took the grove's egress. The daylight was dim, but the rats kept to a clear path, and I espied the small black form weave between the trees and jungle greenery even as it scampered ahead with me following behind.

Not far from the fruit grove, past the foot of a high grassy knoll, stood cave rocks at considerable height. Upon these rocks, a profusion of harried rats scurried up and down the cliffs as if strained under some forced errand at the behest of an unseen master.

Here it was! Multitudes residing therein, nests upon putrid nests! There looked to be several layers of contorted black rock but only one chasmal opening to a subterranean place, mayhap shaped by volcanic lava flows eons ago. The rats had sheltered here from the tropical sun and made this cave their home.

My original scheme was shattered. A lone torch couldn't burn the malign beasts from this underground hollow or even flush them out with billows of smoke. These caves likely extended far down—an unplumbed domain of the rats. And then there may be even more, hidden within secret recesses, skulking like cutpurses within the velvety darkness.

But at least I now knew from whence the rats came. I hoped this was their only lair on this island. How had they arrived here, so far away from Man and his Conurbations which have always sustained these parasitic things? It was a mystery I might solve by searching more of this island, most of it still unknown to me.

Making my way back to the beach dwelling, I espied a lone rat watching me, as one had the previous night. The quarter-sized knave stood on its legs among the bushes, bright eyes gleaming, unafraid even though I was quite close to it. The rat's small brow furrowed unpleasantly as its snout quivered; I even imagined for a moment that the little villain was sneering at me!

Turning purposefully, I left the beast behind, glancing over my shoulder only once to see the rat still watching intently. Could it know where I was going? But how could it? It was but a simple rat and nothing more.

I laid the gourds I had collected from the grove on a plate of palm leaves near the back of my lean-to, my torch beside me. My legs folded, I sat and studied the ocean in the early evening. The tides were rolling in, frothing waves crested with white foam. Was I safe? Dare I sleep tonight, even with an incessant fire shielding my slumbering form?

I realized I needed torches, and many of them. The rats en masse would eventually find me, and I wanted to burn them out before this occurred. Tossing fiery sticks into their dank nests would likely do it, ridding me of the only threat to my safety I knew of.

With the daylight I had left, I scoured the jungle environs for suitable trees (of a heavier sort than the beach palms) with the same urgency with which I had searched for food and water earlier. After some time, I came upon a ridge of verdant hills elevated above the jungle floor. The strapping trees sprouting from these hilltops were noticeably tall, their sweeping branches spread outward in all directions.

Upon reaching the first hilltop, I observed that the trees here had a brownish bark covering their boles, marking their timber as satisfactory as both torchwood as well as for construction of a dwelling if the need came upon me. The fallen branches I gathered were the length of my forearm, and I felt assured these castoffs would make apt incendiary pieces.

But how would these limbs burn for any length of time? A pool of pitch would provide what was necessary, but could one be found? Following the lava-fabricated mountains in the direction of the rat caves, I came upon a gurgling black asphalt seep situated between the hanging cliffs above.

From this heated pool, I coated the top of each branch with the blackish pitch, each wieldy stick of wood now a proper, long-burning torch in the making. The sun set as I spread the torches on flat stones not far from the beach's shore with a mind to permit each torch's pitch overlay to fully dry and thicken. Already humid, I prayed that rain did not come to wash away that for which I had toiled, these makeshift torches my only weapon against a marauding rat horde.

It was dark as I walked to my hut; I would need to claim the finished torches the next morning. Tonight, I would light another fire for protection as I rested. My lean-to on the beach was barely visible under the dim radiance of the moon but, as I approached, the reflecting moonlight exposed the rats, hundreds of them, swarming the place. I was unarmed and now could not return home, my pitch torches not yet prepared.

I fled into the nighttime jungle, unsure of where I might hide but seeing no other recourse. The bright light of the morning sun would likely drive the rats back into their hidey holes, but I needed to survive until then. Once ensconced in their rat den, I would recover my torches and burn the odious bastards without pity!

Running in a direction I hadn't previously sought, I made sure a good distance was between myself and the beach. I then espied and scaled a towering tree, enmeshed in the jungle's packed vegetation.

Supported by its branches and amongst hanging vines, I peered into the night, aided only by the moon overhead. From my vantage point, I saw them. Single file, racing frantically toward my hiding spot above the jungle floor: a line of frenzied rats stretching for some distance.

Knowing rats to be able spoor trackers and climbers, I realized they would find me and be upon me without hesitation. So, crawling across the sturdy branch where I had stood, I then judged the distance to the neighboring tree, its outstretched branches nearly touching my own.

With ropey vines as support, I swung forward, tottering across a lengthy branch of the new tree, before casting myself into an open mud pit near its base. Submerged in muck, I quickly surfaced, wiping my face so my vision was unobscured. I was now bedaubed in the pungent crud, neck deep in the pit's boggy mire.

From down amongst the herbage, I saw a stream of black rats swarming over the branch I had just left. They milled about at the branch's end, seemingly confounded by my absence. A few dropped off, falling onto the jungle floor but no closer to divining my whereabouts. At last, the little fiends had lost my trail!

The thick muck encasement clung to me as a limpet does to a tidal rock, masking my scent from the prowling rats. I pulled myself into the waiting ferns, creeping from the mud pit, the dark of night hiding my prone form. I waited until I could no longer hear the chirping of the rats and then stood to make my way into the jungle's foreboding interior.

The still sound of the jungle under a hidden moon embraced my ears, the quietness making me fearful, as if my sharp-set foe were lying in wait. Every rustle of a plant, every shadow at my outer vision, every susurrant breeze amongst the trees seemed to presage an attack by the rats, who had found me despite my efforts to elude them. I continued on in this way for some time until I saw what I thought could be the island's north shore, far from the nesting rats and their warrens.

A spreading knot of island trees awaited me, their fan-shaped fronds swaying in nocturnal winds without companions on a high, grassy mound. Waves crashed over the beach not far from where I scaled to a place of repose, huddling myself within the bough of the palm trees' surging stems.

Far off, I could hear the rats' tremulous twittering; it was as if they were calling to one another. Would they espy me in my safe haven? I had to chance sleep, praying my blessed Savior would guard me against these devils as I lay vulnerable. The rats' gnashing teeth setting upon my tired limbs entered my mind as I drifted out of consciousness, but the weight of slumber was too much to bear...

I blinked in the morning sunlight, relieved as I opened my eyes to a tranquil, sandy-white shore under the ocean's horizon. I had survived the night unscathed.

Now, with a clear view of the island's northernmost beach, I saw a great hull of a galleon, its masts rotted and broken, a toppled behemoth lying on its side in shallow waters. I shimmied down the palm trees' stems, landing on my feet, and then walked to the beach to examine the shipwreck.

The shattered hulk was perhaps a century or more in age, I surmised, likely part of an *armada* that had explored these islands long ago. The rats must have come from this woeful wreckage, the ship's only survivors after nearly breaking apart amongst the shore's rocky outcroppings.

Still caked in a muddy shroud, I fell into the tides around the ship, washing away that which had concealed me the previous night. Sea water dripped from what remained of my tattered clothing as I strode ashore, confident my garments would dry in the hot sun.

Shielding my eyes with a hand as I stood on dry land, I scoured the lonely littoral, empty save for the enormous flotsam of the ruined ship. I espied what seemed to be the mouth of a cave embedded in a craggy, barren cliff face. Was this a place of the rats as well? I doubted it; the cave was too close to the sea.

I walked along the beach until I met the cave's entrance. The cave appeared shallow when I looked in from the mouth but may still have provided shelter to someone. The vanquished galleon could have washed living souls ashore after all.

Within, not far from the opening, were signs of occupation, but not recent. The emaciated bones of a man, doubtless the only survivor of the galleon's crew, rested on a bed of withered fronds at the cave's back. The sorrowful remains bore the rags of a *conquistador*'s finery, clinging to him even after many years in deathly solitude.

I found an iron axe, pitted and rusted to uselessness; hooks for fishing; and evidence that wood had been hewn within the cave. Outside, under the shelter of the rocky cliffs, a braced wooden raft lay flush against the cliff walls. The raft had been purposely hidden with foliage, but now only desiccated remnants of those jungle plants covered its bare planks.

If, perhaps, sinewy vines were to replace the decaying rope lashed between the raft's logs for reinforcement, the raft might still be usable. Here it was, my means of escape from this accursed island of shipwrecks! I needed only gather those vines, bind them to the raft, and then drag the seaworthy vessel into the waters off these shores. I could be cresting the ocean waves by the next sunrise!

I labored during the sweltering day in the jungle close to the beach, knowing hunger and thirst but carried aloft by the prospect of my looming freedom. I now had enough strong, fibrous vines to fortify the raft, ensuring her log beams would remain together during my trip over deep waters.

Working quickly, I tied the vines to the raft's logs, fastening them taut. I would only know if the raft was truly seaworthy once pushed out into the ocean, but that would need wait. The rats! Their numbers must be culled before I left this island.

These creatures were clearly abominations, gifted with some strange intelligence, perhaps even diabolical in nature. I knew I should put them to the flame, leaving none alive if within my power to do so. All I had seen was the Hand of Lucifer at work. Cleansing this place of his evil was my blest duty as a Follower of Christ.

I found the pool of refreshing water near the grove of the gourd fruits after travelling back from the north of the island. I drank for some time and then rested on the wet sand, hoping the remaining daylight was enough for my task. I gathered gourds from the grove and ate several of them, knowing I would be able to carry scarcely any food with me when I returned to my raft.

The pitch torches I had prepared were undisturbed, lying in a row on the flat rocks where I had left them. Palm fronds and loose branches were a burden but I collected as many as I could, holding them in my outstretched arms as I advanced toward the lava caves of the rats.

These terrible vermin feared the pure sun and, on this day, the tranquil blue sky over the island was empty of clouds. Cloistered in their sunless cavern, the rats would be roasted alive in their foul lair—but, first, I had to plumb its depths. With a heap of kindling near the cave's mouth, I entered, a solitary torch lighting my way as I trod along dark paths.

The light from the sun outside was soon swallowed up by the darkness of the cave. My torch blazed, casting outlandish shadows about the walls as I took deliberate steps. I caught the faint echoes of scuttling and the chirping of rats, the contours of a darting form sometimes appearing large against the earthen passageway into which I progressed.

As I moved farther into the caves, the stone walls glistened as if coated with a sickening, oily lubricant. I held my torch to the wall closest and noted a thin black ooze of sorts covering much of its surface. It rippled ever so slightly as if in response to the heat of the torchlight.

These caves could go very deep indeed, I realized, even into the bowels of the World herself, this island being only the fertile top of an expansive mountain reaching out beyond the waves and into the vast ocean. Whatever was here could be quite ancient, from a time before Man ever sailed the seas or even strode upon the good soil of Our Lord's Creation.

The long passage seemed to come to an end and another arched opening appeared in the stone of the cave not far ahead of me. I stepped through and found a narrow ledge, the precarious cusp of a spiraling pit. Beneath my feet, I looked down, my torch illuminating a sight of unspeakable horror.

A seething, undulating mass of black fur and open jaws filled the pit below, the many hundreds of rats clawing over each other, ensnarled in a twisted web of rattish carnality. Something fell from the cave ceiling above and landed on the ledge close by to me, momentarily pulling my eyes from the horror in the pit.

I held my torch over what had fallen, my vision limited in this abyssal recess. It was a black glob near to the size of my hand, its substance alike to what I had seen on the passage walls leading to this place. Again, as with the slimes along the walls of the passageway, the glob appeared to recoil under my burning torch, its lacquered skin perturbed by the torch's wounding flames.

My head tilted upward and I saw from whence the strange blob had come: the stone ceiling above the rat pit was overspread with the black goo, its moist folds surging, the otherworldly, putrescent grot ebbing and flowing around lava-formed stalactites, born of a molten inferno.

The hand-sized glob at my foot then crept away, crawling up the walls of the cave to meld with the cowl of cascading ooze hanging over me. The black slime was alive, feeding on or even guiding the rats below it. The rats had bred here in the unseen entrails of the cave's deepest part, shaped and nurtured by an alien intellect dredged from within the Earth's antediluvian crust.

I ran from the disgusting pit, the withering flames from my dying torch leading me back to sunlight and my bunches of kindling. I took to the task of piling the wood and fronds into the passage leading back to that place, praying the fire and smoke would kill the Hell-spawned rats and the Hadean monstrosity that festered above them.

The chirping of the rats grew into a great tumult as I piled the last of the tinder onto the heap; perhaps the subterrene entity had warned them of my intent, the aberration sensing the thoughts and animus of those around it. Torch after pitch torch—I tossed them one after the other into the now burning accumulation.

Panic-stricken rats had begun to emerge into the passage-way when I flung the final torch onto the freshly blazing bonfire. Without hesitation, I charged toward the cave's entrance, charred vapors from the rats' funeral pyre smothering the tunnelways I had left behind me.

There, in the bright light of the sun, I watched as pillars of choking black smoke issued forth from the cave's stony orifice, the horrible shrieking of the rats manifest even from the cliffs where I stood. The fiends were done, painfully suffocated in their loathsome and abysmal demesne.

I resolved to make my journey over the ocean that night, not wishing to linger much longer. That I would be able to subsist on rainwater and the raw fish of the sea was my hope. I prospected a miserable death by starvation or thirst, but I could no longer remain on this friendless island, cast away from those I loved and from all that my heart held most dear.

My raft rested above the rolling waves near the shore, bobbing steadily on the limpid ocean waters of the shoal. The gourds I had would nourish me for a few days, and I had taken the fishing hooks from the cave of the *conquistador* with but sparse jungle vines to thread them.

The sun was starting to set. Wanting to forage the *conquistador*'s cave a final time, I yearned for the chance of procuring something to aid my trip. Not much light was left for this day, but the cave was small and by now I knew it well.

I searched through the back of the cave, my eyes squinting in the dismal light. Under a reddish stone was a depthless crevice, not much deeper than the length of my hand. In it rested a bundle of brass twine, attendant cords for the *conquistador*'s fishing hooks! Hidden well—the man must have made use of the twine only when it had been truly needed.

I heard a squeak from somewhere behind me. Soon, more sharp, high-pitched squeaks followed. I turned to find the shapes of many rats gathered in the shadows of the cave's threshold.

Running, I leapt over the teeming rats who had gathered to block my way, but hundreds more were outside. How had they escaped? At least some should have perished in the caves but there must have been legions more of these black furry devils emplaced elsewhere.

Rats clambered up all sides of my exposed leg, hissing as they bit and scratched. The pain from the small bites and claws was dull, but I knew I was in grave danger. The thronging rats would devour me, leaving not a morsel, if they managed to bring me to ground.

Violently shaking them loose, the rats scattered as I lunged across the beach and dove into the waters close to my raft. I pulled myself aboard, clutching the brass twine from the cave. Having contrived an oar from a heavy tree branch, I paddled mightily, guiding the raft over the tumbling waves and out to sea.

The rats gave dogged pursuit, swimming into the ocean and scrambling onto the raft's stern. I swung in an arch, swatting them with my oar, sending some flying back into the water while others were crushed into bloody heaps. Along the beach, I espied a large form, striding head and haunches above the innumerable rats that still milled about onshore.

The thing I saw was a monstrous black rat with the immensity of a wolfhound, the apparent king of the assembled mass. The Rat King's eyes overflowed with the same black ooze I had seen on the walls of the rat pit, as if the thinking filth had taken this rat as its vessel and then had grown it to a preternatural size.

The Rat King, its eyes black-within-black, stood up on its hind legs as it saw me. Dominant over its teeming minions, the aberrant beast let out an unspeakable roar as I sailed into the red sun of day's end, buoyed by the rising tide out to sea. I had denied the beast its prey, perchance avoiding the fate of possession, through which I would doubtless have been taken into the viscous folds of a horror from the very depths of the Netherworld itself.

The dying sun finally slept and I lay upon my raft, the ocean waves beneath me chopping over its sides. As I drifted over the dark waters, I prayed to Our Lord and Savior that I would soon be found and that these strange rats and their subterranean master would remain on their forsaken island, where Man may never again encounter them.

The Empress

The bell chimed musically as Felix stood back on the
steps, waiting for a reply. The embellished mahogany
door soon swung inward and a woman appeared under the
arched entryway, a spotted silver and gray cat in her arms.
She smiled warmly for a moment and then said, "Come in,"
with a welcoming gesture.

Walking into her well-appointed home from the spacious
foyer, Felix followed the woman inside. The woman's cat
sprang from her arms to the richly carpeted floor as they entered the hallway, promptly disappearing down an adjoining
side hall.

The two-story house was stately and Victorian, even im-
posing from outside on the street. Felix had gulped and then
rung the doorbell after walking up a long, winding flight of
steps to the front door, not entirely sure who would answer
his call.

The woman was pearl blonde and hazel eyed, her long
hair set into a neat bun at the back of her head. She was
likely middle-aged but still seemed youthful, even alluringly
beautiful, as an older woman. Dressed quite formally, the
woman's clothing appeared old-fashioned to Felix, almost
as if she was wearing a stylish ensemble from another era.

The two entered an open parlor room decorated with rare
antiquities and artwork from the past. A round burnished
table matched with two high-backed chairs stood off to the

room's side, some distance from the middle. Fresh red and white roses were arranged in a cut-jade vase hanging from the wall closest to the table, their heady fragrance noticeable as soon as Felix reached the room's center.

The woman turned to Felix and requested, "Please take a seat at the divination table," indicating the room's corner spot. "I'll be back in one moment with refreshments for both of us. Feel free to look around in the meantime and be sure to make yourself at home."

Felix casually observed the woman exit to another room and then studied the parlor's walls and shelves, examining the curios decorating the place. In particular, he noticed the gold mask of a cat in the style of ancient Egypt mounted to a wall space, set among other antiquarian guises. The mask seemed a genuine artifact crafted from real gold and not some cheap fabrication one might see as part of a theatrical costume.

Returning with a tea set on a polished pewter tray after some time, the woman placed the tray on the bare wood surface between the table's two upholstered chair. She poured hot tea into a porcelain cup and then seated herself across from Felix, who was now resting comfortably against his chair's plush back.

"My name is Sophia," the woman said brightly, showing her warm smile once again. "I sincerely apologize for the delayed introduction."

Felix reached over to lightly shake her outstretched hand. "Felix," he said, taking his teacup afterward. "My sister Celeste urged me to come and see you. I've been having odd dreams lately and my sister is convinced you can tell me about these dreams. But I'll let you know: I'm skeptical myself."

"That's your right, of course," Sophia replied, her voice reassuring. "And, yes, Celeste called and told me you'd be stopping by soon for a reading. You're just as handsome as she said you'd be." She smiled again, but her smile was different, even a bit sly.

Felix blushed unconsciously, which was quite unlike him; he was always anchored and self-confident, especially around women. But something was enticing to Felix about Sophia, even though he thought she might be twice his age or perhaps even older. *She must have been an exceptional beauty in her younger days*, Felix thought wistfully, *the center of men's attention.*

The spotted silver-gray cat appeared from behind Sophia's chair and crawled into her lap with a jump. Purring contentedly as the animal settled in, the silky coated feline curled into a tight ball, its head tucked under its banded tail, before training its acute gaze on Felix.

The cat watched Felix intently from its resting spot as if it was somehow scrutinizing him from across the table. *Impossible*, thought Felix, slightly unnerved by this unexpected behavior from the clairvoyant's loyal companion. *It's only a cat.*

"Celeste told me that you're a card reader, that you tell fortunes," Felix continued, pulling his eyes away from the puzzling cat and back to Sophia. "She said that the cards have meaning, meaning that might be connected to my dreams?"

"All the cards have a certain meaning," Sophia said, nodding as she spoke. "Whether their meaning is connected to your dreams is another matter. But first, I'll perform a reading and let the cards tell us your story."

Drinking from his teacup, Felix watched Sophia spread a deck of cards out on the table between them. Each card had a curious figure or scene displayed on its face, none of which Felix recognized.

Looking back at Felix, Sophia began discussing the cards and their purpose. "The cards of the major arcana have pictures representing various forces, characters, virtues, and vices," she explained, speaking as if she were narrating a story to a friend. "One card represents yours or another's past, the next card represents sometime in the present, and the final card in the three-card spread is a future... again, yours or someone else's. We may see something here or we may not."

Sophia shuffled and fanned out the deck face down in front of Felix, with only the backs of the cards now visible. "Pull a card from the deck. Whichever one you feel most drawn to. Fate will guide your hand to the first card."

"But I can't see which cards are which now," Felix objected, bewildered by what seemed like showy but pointless subterfuge. "How do I know what I'm picking?"

Seemingly frustrated, Sophia countered and said, "You don't. That's the point. Your soul will be the one to draw a card, not your eyes. Now pick."

Unsure of what this increasingly baffling woman could mean, Felix drew a face-down card near the spread's center. He looked at his choice and then placed the card on the table with its image facing Sophia.

"The Fool," Sophia stated, apparently pleased by the gaudily colored court jester displayed on the card. "This card represents bright beginnings, perhaps something in your early life. Have you had any dreams about your past that this card might represent?"

"No... not that I can recall," Felix answered, not altogether certain. "But you said a card can be about someone else's past, not just mine."

Sophia looked at Felix earnestly for a moment as if searching for some insight and then said, "I have something that should help us."

Leaving the cat on the floor, Sophia took the pewter tray from the reading table and disappeared into the neighboring room. Some time passed, and Felix heard nothing. It was as if Sophia had departed from this mortal coil and entered the spirit world.

Sophia's cat rested near her empty chair and watched Felix with the same intent as before, purring quietly. The cat licked its paw and then scurried off into the room that Sophia had entered from the parlor.

My dreams—nightmares really—I think one of them was about a cat, Felix thought to himself while Sophia's pet departed. *I can't really remember now.*

Sophia suddenly walked in, carrying a quartz glass sphere on an elaborate bronze stand. The metallic brown stand had lost its luster long ago and looked very old, as if the object had been passed down to her through many ages.

Placing the crystal ball on the table before Felix, Sophia sat across from him again. The cat was nowhere to be seen.

"What's your cat's name, if I may ask?" Felix said politely as his eyes searched the room for the cat, unsure if he had ever seen this breed.

"Oh, her name is Bastet. But I just call her Bast." Sophia smiled and regarded the ball with delight, deliberately passing her hands over the sparkling clear orb on the stand between them in sweeping gestures.

"You honestly believe we can see the future with that museum piece?" Felix asked dubiously as he observed Sophia, briefly extending a hand toward the crystal ball before quickly withdrawing it.

"It's much more than a relic from antiquity," Sophia replied, not bothering to chide Felix for his tactless remark about a tool of her trade. "And not just the future, Felix, but also the past. Your past... or the past of someone else."

As Sophia's hands moved just over the crystalline ball's surface, its core became cloudy, steadily filling with billowing gray mists. Now brumous and opaque, Sophia removed her hands from the ball.

She said, "Peer closely into the swirling center of the sphere." The afternoon's natural light seemed to dim and the room became shadowy as Felix focused on the mystical orb before him. "Hold your gaze until your mind's eye perceives what the Other World has chosen to show us."

Felix blinked and stared fixedly into the mists, momentarily wondering what he had gotten himself into. *Is this all a parlor trick?* he thought, disappointed; he had wasted a Saturday driving across town. *This ball is only a prop, I bet. Purchased from a pawn shop somewhere. It's all just theater for the rubes.*

Sophia's voice became ever more distant, as if she was now far away and calling to Felix instead of just speaking to him. Shapes began to appear within the crystal ball, at first indistinct but then more defined. Stone pyramids over a desert, the pillars of a temple, and then the majestic statue of a goddess of cats. Men moved about the opulent temple to the cat deity, her favored felines their companions.

The Fool Card—A Past

Neferkare sat at his simple cedar desk with a wet reed brush, his scribe's work before him. He had been tasked with recording the daily activities of the temple's novice scribes, acolytes, priests, and other functionaries on papyrus scrolls. A ledger was also kept of the alms given to the Temple of Bastet by the pious, as the temple had many devoted followers outside of its walls in the surrounding city.

Finishing his last entry for the night, Neferkare prepared to leave his chamber adjoining the temple library. He thought back to the serene waters flowing past the palm-lined, sandy banks around the temple's island home, a tranquil oasis in the middle of its river.

Earlier that evening, Neferkare had been outside the temple walls to clear his burdened mind and had noted the nighttime scenery. The luminescent moon had been drifting through the cloudy skies overhead, the stars faint but still visible, and the eternal Nile calm and steady, sustaining the lives of his people.

I should check on Dedi as it's bedtime, *thought the tired priest.* He'll want his saucer of milk before sleep.

Making his way down a dark temple hallway lit only by a few hanging oil lamps, Neferkare searched for his cat. Long shadows scattered as Neferkare turned a sharp corner and saw Dedi, seemingly waiting for him at the other end of the hall.

"There you are, my good friend," Neferkare said aloud, his words echoing in the otherwise silent temple hall. "Come, I'll bring you to the kitchen for milk and perhaps a treat."

Stepping forward, Neferkare strode with purpose toward the spotted silver-gray cat, intent on scooping him up in his arms. The cat, however, quickly dodged as Neferkare approached, disappearing into the dimly lit hall nearby.

"Dedi is skittish tonight," Neferkare remarked to himself. "That's so unlike him. He knows that it's time for his milk and catnip. I wonder what might have gotten into him."

Neferkare turned right and saw someone standing not far from him in the adjacent hallway, waiting in the gloomy shadows. The figure held Dedi in its arms, the cat now purring but with a hint of menace.

"Who is that?" Neferkare called out, but not too loudly, for he did not wish to awaken the sleeping priests and acolytes. "Is that you, Senbi? If you need more scrolls from the library, it can wait until the morning."

Dedi hissed and leaped from the arms of the stranger onto the stone floor before sprinting out of sight. The robed figure rushed forward in an instant, cutting short Neferkare's terrified scream.

Frantic shadows danced along the walls of the temple hall as the two combatants struggled, the silhouette of a drawn dagger evident. Then, at once, a gust of wind snuffed out the flickering lights of the hanging lamps, shrouding all in a cloak of darkness.

Ameny stood at the banks of the Nile and looked out over its turbid gray-green waters, wondering where Neferkare might be. The morning sun had risen and the bustle of the city around them could now be seen from the temple.

Neferkare must have crept away into the city, *Ameny thought to himself amusedly.* Perhaps he has a woman there.

Taking his water jug, Ameny walked to the well outside the temple walls. He lowered the bucket and filled his jug to its brim. He would keep the jug in his quarters as he had been quite thirsty recently. Why, he couldn't say.

The acolyte Qebu passed Ameny as he started up the steps to the broad colonnaded facade that made up the temple's entrance. Shielding his eyes from the sun with a hand, the young man paused and called out to him.

"Brother Ameny, please do not enter the temple now," he said, his voice almost shaking. "A terrible crime has been committed, which you do not wish to see."

"What crime, Brother Qebu?" Ameny replied, concerned. "What is so terrible that I cannot lay my eyes upon it?"

"A murder, my brother," said Qebu, his face pained as he spoke. "The murder of a priest of this temple. Brother Neferkare is dead."

Two more acolytes hurried past Ameny and Qebu, briefly glancing at them but plainly distracted and distraught. Ameny began to walk back up the temple steps. "I should witness what has happened, Qebu," Ameny said, turning as he made his way upward. "Brother Neferkare was as dear to me as a father is to a son. I must know how he died."

Standing between two monolithic red granite columns, Ameny assessed the open floors of the temple before him. Acolytes hastened about its interior, weaving among the many cats, the animal sacred to Bastet, Her most favored. But no sign of a death. Ameny decided he must search within the temple instead.

The bright morning sun gave way to cool shadows as Ameny ducked into one of the side halls leading to the temple library. Voices

86

echoed through the hallway. The faint smell of blood hung in the air as Ameny walked forward.

Near the hall's end, Ameny saw what appeared to be a prone body veiled with a darkly stained cloth not far from him. Several priests watched over the anonymous corpse, which he right away thought must be that of Neferkare.

Senusret, the temple's high priest, locked eyes with Ameny, noticing his presence among them. "Come no further, Ameny," he commanded, firm in his authority. "Brother Neferkare was found like this shortly after sunrise. We may all be in danger from whoever committed this foul deed. Death stalks these halls."

The vigilant priests put themselves between Ameny and the crime scene, forcing him to step back. "Yes, High Priest Senusret," Ameny responded, obedient. "I will do as you say. The temple has been told of what has transpired here?"

"Of course... soon," Senusret answered, taking a long breath, grieved and nearly spent. "We will gather all our brothers in the garden under the palms at midday and let them know of this wicked act. We are taking Neferkare's remains into the tombs now."

Ameny left his deceased friend and mentor, exiting toward the temple's exterior. Clusters of acolytes were huddling across the multi-tiled floors behind the façade's pillars, murmuring to each other fearfully. Word must have spread very quickly of Neferkare's death, even as the scores of Bastet's faithful had gone about their duties.

Who could have killed such a man? *Ameny thought, seized with unease at the idea that the murderer wasn't yet finished.* Neferkare had no enemies. He was like a father to many younger priests, including myself. He was among Bastet's most devout. *Ameny needed to be in the library soon for his duties as a scribe, but he decided to visit his room first with the water jug.*

As Ameny shifted the jug's weight in his hands, a temple cat leaped onto the pedestal of a stone statue of Bastet nearby. Ameny turned, noticing he was being observed with great interest. The cat's fur had charcoal-gray spots covering its silver coat, a characteristic shared by all of the temple's many cats.

"Most beloved of Bastet," Ameny said, taking a few steps forward. "Midday nears; shouldn't you be at the cattery? Here, let me help you back and find you a saucer of milk."

The cat began yowling frantically as Ameny approached, making long, drawn-out howls rapidly and in succession as if raising an alarm. Then, the cat stopped abruptly, jumping to the floor and scurrying away into the inner temple.

What could have gotten into him? Ameny thought, thoroughly bemused. We are the doting servants of the cats, Bastet's sacred creatures. Did something frighten him, or was he trying to warn me? About what?

Someone was standing behind him. Ameny turned and saw the head scribe, Minhotep, his eyes boring into him. Ameny was the man's apprentice and the stern Minhotep seemed to watch Ameny's every movement during the day.

"Why are you not at your scribe's desk, Brother Ameny?" Minhotep inquired, his hands laid across his arms, swathed in the white robes of his station. "You should be working on the scrolls I provided to you. I need them today, at once." Minhotep scowled in disapproval at his charge, the leathery skin around his thin lips creasing as he did.

"I am so sorry, Head Scribe Minhotep," Ameny said in deference, apologizing profusely. "I fetched this jug of water for my room and was headed to the library. But do you not know what happened to Brother Neferkare?"

Minhotep relaxed slightly, feeling his neophyte was no longer challenging his authority. "No," he replied. "I heard some commotion this morning but I've been working in my chambers since sunrise. Has Brother Neferkare fallen ill?"

Ameny hesitated, cautious of how Minhotep might react. "Neferkare is dead—murdered," he replied, guarded. "Senusret will gather all at midday to tell the entire temple. In preparation for *the afterlife, Neferkare's body is to be kept in the catacombs before mummification."*

Furrowing his brow, Minhotep gasped. "May Bastet protect us!" he cried, forcefully throwing his hands in the air. "Is the killer still among us?"

"No one knows," Ameny replied, still unsure of his often-mercurial master. "Senusret believes we may all be in danger. We'll know more later today when he speaks in the garden under the palms."

Minhotep struggled to regain his composure, badly shaken by this news, but he did not wish to appear fearful before his apprentice. "Take your water jug to your cell and then come to the library," he instructed, now calm. "I will inform the other scribes—that is, if they do not know of our Brother Neferkare's fate by now."

After leaving Minhotep, Ameny entered his scribe's cell near the hall of priests' chambers. The small room was sparse; its only fur-nishings consisted of a woven reed mat covered with linen sheets and a low cedar wood table, onto which he placed his water jug.

A few papyrus scrolls also lay on the table; Ameny had taken them from the temple library yesterday in the early evening for study. Scrolls weren't supposed to be removed from the library, but he doubted Minhotep would notice, at least not right away. The scrolls had been left on Ameny's work desk by someone unknown.

Ameny opened one of the scrolls and read from its hieratic script, written in the archaic manner of the Old Kingdom:

Beware of the One from the Night of Shadows, the One who Dwells in the Uninviting Desert. For She is the Corrup-tor of all Pure Souls, the Deceiver who Lies and Tempts those who Seek Undeserved Power...

Even having examined other library scrolls from the same period, Ameny still was unsure what this meant. The vast desert to the south was largely unexplored as it was so desolate. Could something be lurking there that threatened Bastet and Her disciples? Ameny couldn't say.

Yet scrolls from the Old Kingdom I have not seen might reveal more, *he thought. But Ameny suspected that Minhotep may be hiding such scrolls somewhere, maybe in the temple's recesses or perhaps underground in the catacombs?*

After drinking from his water jug, Ameny went to the library and sat at his scribe's desk, finding more scrolls waiting for him. Minhotep was very demanding of his scribes, but Ameny was always able to keep pace with his master's sometimes almost impossible requests. Scholarly and exacting, he was a practiced scrivener, proficient in both hieroglyphic and hieratic writing.

Ameny opened a new scroll and found it had already been transcribed, even though his reed brush was dry. What is this? *he thought.* The writing is not fresh either; the opposite really.

Scanning its columns, Ameny concluded this scroll was from the same series as those left for him previously. The first part of the ancient text read:

Those who Seek Power will Turn on their Brothers, Placing Hubris and Conceit above all other Things. They will Strike when Those who Put their Trust in Them least Expect it...

Footsteps behind Ameny prompted him to roll the scroll closed, brushing away a few loose cat hairs before putting it under his desk. Minhotep stood before him.

"Ameny, I have more work for you once you are finished with those," Minhotep said, glancing at the remaining scrolls on this desk. "The devotional liturgies of Bastet require the utmost diligence from Her anointed scribes. Of that, you have my confidence." Minhotep smiled for a moment, which was uncharacteristic of him, and then walked away. Ameny heard him speaking in a low voice to another scribe somewhere behind the wide shelves of scrolls.

Preserving the knowledge of centuries, the temple library was a repository of the past, and not all of it was religious in nature.

It was midday, and the ascendant sun baked the open garden behind the temple with its stark heat, the garden's many palm trees casting dappled shade. Senusret stood on the raised steps leading to the temple's antecedent doors, hands at his waist as he looked out over the priests and acolytes assembled before him. Satisfied everyone was present, Senusret cleared his throat and began to speak.

"Servants of Bastet," Senusret said, greeting his audience in a ringing voice. "One of our number has fallen to violence. Brother Neferkare's lifeless body was found in the temple halls this morning at sunrise, lying in a pool of his own blood. Who could have committed such an act is not known, but we will find them, especially if they are among our ranks. Bastet will have Her vengeance, I promise you."

A murmur rippled through the crowd, growing louder as their fear became palpable. Who would lay a hand on one of Bastet's holy clergy? The people of the Nile revered the denizens of Bastet's temple, with the temple grounds and its island considered sacred. To them, Bastet's priest class was untouchable.

The acolyte Qebu was the first to speak out. "High Priest Senusret, what can we, the faithful of Bastet, do?" he asked pleadingly. "Where do we search? Who do we question?" Other acolytes and priests called out in clamorous agreement, demanding swift retribution for the murder of a temple priest.

Senusret raised his arms over his head, the palms of his hands facing outward. "Brothers, there are no witnesses," he told the crowd. "This terrible deed occurred in the dead of night, under the light of an oil lamp. But, this night, I will burn incense and give sacrifice to Bastet, performing an augur. May the Goddess grant me second sight and reveal to me the murderer of Her devoted servant."

A murmur again spread through the crowd, the priests and acolytes placated—at least for the time being. The outcome of Senusret's augury would be revealed tomorrow, likely at midday, as had been today's address. What might Goddess Bastet send to him? Silence would be the worst outcome of all, telling the Goddess's adherents that they had been abandoned in a time of crisis.

Leaving the palm gardens, Ameny drew water from the well as he had at sunrise. The well's waters were replenished from the two canals flowing around the temple's island, fed from the Nile itself and ending in an underground basin.

Ameny placed his water jug along the stone ledge and lowered the hanging bucket into the well's cool, aphotic depths. The well was deep and the rope suspending the bucket had begun to fray. It would need to be replaced soon.

Ameny thought of the priests and acolytes and how the men had reacted to Senusret's disclosure of a killing within their closed religious community. No temple occupant had borne any wrath toward Neferkare, or at least none that Ameny knew of. So, who could be the perpetrator then?

The Temple to Bastet was on a delta within the River Nile, accessible only by bridge, the waters nearby swarming with hungry Nile crocodiles. A high wall also surrounded the temple grounds, almost impossible to climb over without detection by the night watch. Unless the temple guard was somehow compromised, no one could have entered from the outside to commit the murder of Neferkare.

Bastet may tell us if She is listening, *Ameny thought, his mood pensive, almost melancholy. In the past, the divinations of Senusret's auguries had often been vague, more subjective interpretations than divine revelation. But this was the first time a priest had fallen to violence in the temple itself, something heretofore unheard of, even in past ages. Bastet could perhaps intervene with a potent insight for Her high priest.*

Leaving behind a full jug of water on his cell table, Ameny returned to his place in the library. The scrolls were gone, including the cryptic scroll from the Old Kingdom he had deposited under his scribe's desk when Minhotep had checked on him.

Looking around, Ameny worried that Minhotep had taken them. He hurried back to his cell and found the other scrolls gone, retrieved from under the table where they had been stashed.

No one is allowed to enter my cell except the high priest, *Ameny thought, panicking.* Once someone notices the scrolls missing, Minhotep will start to accuse the scribes, including me.

Holding out hope that the scrolls might be on the library shelves, Ameny returned, searching the stacks piled with papyrus rolled on wooden sticks. Two novice scribes were conversing nearby, not noticing Ameny as he hid behind a shelf to listen.

"They say Senusret is the one behind it," the first novice whispered, nervous about being overheard. "Something has corrupted him, they say, something quite dark."

The second novice replied quietly. "Like what? You mean an evil spirit? The wandering wastes of the southern desert are supposed to be haunted with them."

"Perhaps, but perhaps something even worse," the first novice suggested, his voice falling lower. "There are stories of a she-demon from the lands north between the rivers. But this demon haunts the deserts of our lands now, searching for a foothold into the world of those who are awake but still dream. She comes to those she wishes to corrupt in dreams, tempting those who yearn for power."

An uncanny rush of wind surged through the library, fluttering scraps of parchment left on the scribes' desks. Almost jolted from his hiding spot by the disturbance, Ameny felt a chill shadow come over him, a biting shudder seizing him as it did. The abnormal shadow then ebbed, receding behind the scroll-laden shelves. The two novices had ceased talking.

Senusret again held his hands toward the crowd gathered in the garden under the palms at midday. The priests and acolytes were waiting to hear what his augur to Bastet had revealed about the murder of Brother Neferkare.

Ameny was among the crowd, having dodged Minhotep that morning when his master had gone looking for him. Minhotep was nowhere to be seen now.

"Faithful of Bastet…" Senusret declared, but this first utterance was cut short. A sudden rush of wind appeared from nowhere, blowing through the crowd and about Senusret, then disappearing almost as quickly as it had come. Senusret's expression became strange, even poisonous, for a moment before he turned toward his priesthood to speak.

"Brothers," he exclaimed in a commanding voice, both arms extended outward. "The Goddess has blessed us and shared a vision. There is a malevolent presence in Bastet's holy temple! It is the Great Serpent, Apep, the adversary of our Goddess and the Father of All Creation, Ra. Neferkare, to my sorrow, was struck down because he had lost his faith in our Mother, Bastet."

A wave of distress washed over those gathered at this terrible revelation. An acolyte then cried out, his fist raised in the air, "We must make sacrifice to appease Bastet and drive this evil from our midst! It is the only way."

Other acolytes and many priests nodded and shouted in agreement, demanding that any agents of Apep be found at once.

"But High Priest Senusret," inquired the priest Senbi hesitantly. "What assassin drove his dagger into Brother Neferkare? If Apep is behind all of this, who was his hand?"

"No one," replied Senusret, unflinching and steadfast. "The vision I received from Bastet showed but a black snake of smoke coiled around the neck of our Brother Neferkare before it struck with its bite. He was felled entirely by supernatural means. Our only recourse is to pray and hope that Bastet protects us. I will offer sacrifice to Bastet and hope She forgives our transgression."

The priests and acolytes muttered among themselves and then dispersed, returning to their daily tasks. Senusret watched from the temple steps as the crowd melted away, his piercing eyes darkly shaded with kohl. The gardens seemed empty when Senusret finally left, sidestepping into a postern entrance to the temple not far away.

Ameny had surveilled Senusret as the others departed, secreted behind a lofty date palm, its pale green fronds swaying in the Nile's breeze. Senusret went out of sight as he re-entered the temple; Ameny knew where he'd be.

Once in the hallway, Ameny caught a glimpse of Senusret disappearing around a corner. He was headed for the high priest's sanctum; he was almost certain of that. Perhaps to meet someone there?

A door closed and Ameny turned into the now empty hall. He crept quietly toward the high priest's sanctum, hearing voices as he pressed himself close to the door, its ornate wood surface painted in bright colors.

"Tonight is a new moon," the first voice said, its owner's identity unclear. "We can wait no longer. She grows impatient. This sacred place of Bastet must be Hers, to mold, to corrupt."

The second voice interrupted: "We have brought over enough acolytes. Now is the time." This was likely Senusret. "The danger lies with the remaining priests who still worship Bastet. They may be too strong to bring down all at once. Neferkare was but a loose end; he had learned too much."

Both voices paused, and there were footsteps toward the door. Ameny quickly ducked around the nearby corner and briskly walked down the adjoining hallway, turning once to ensure he wasn't being followed.

We have been infiltrated by unbelievers, *Ameny thought, now frightened of what might transpire soon.* Senusret has a co-conspirator. But who? And who can I tell without proof? I risk my life by accusing Bastet's high priest of apostasy.

Ameny lay on his reed mat, his cell dark and quiet. He believed all were asleep now save for those in the night watch, which patrolled the temple grounds until dawn. The temple cats were active at night but mostly in their cattery, rarely leaving the temple.

Turning on his side, Ameny couldn't find rest. He'd been afraid to tell anyone what he had heard at the high priest's sanctum, not knowing who he could trust.

Minhotep? No, he'd probably be given a sound thrashing just for the accusation against Senusret. And it was odd that Minhotep was still absent; he'd not been seen in the library since the morning.

His fellow scribes? Again, no. How many acolytes had been "brought over," and to what?

His eyes half open, Ameny heard the soft tapping of footsteps against stone outside the door to his cell. As a scribe to Minhotep, Ameny was permitted his own room while most other acolytes slept together in a single chamber with little privacy. The acolytes' chamber was not far from Ameny's cell and was along the same temple hall.

Breaking the near silence, there was a sudden cry and then shouting from several voices, followed by the sounds of frantic fighting in the halls. The light from a blazing torch threw shadows under the threshold of Ameny's cell door, and more panicked shouting and cries rang out as the torch's illumination receded.

"Mother Bastet," Ameny murmured, pushing aside his sheets and rising from his mat. "Are we under attack?"

As Ameny stood, the door to his cell swung open. The silhouette of a figure blocked the doorway, even as acolytes in the hall ran past. The room was dark, but Ameny could tell it was another acolyte. It was Qebu.

*"Well, Little Brother, are you ready to meet the Great Mother?"
Qebu asked, his lips baring a wolfish smile as the dim outline of his
face became visible.*

*Ameny took a step back but Qebu struck without warning. Ameny
felt something solid hit him sharply on the head, and he fell against
a wall, sliding down, a torpid blackness closing in.*

*A taste of blood in his mouth, Ameny came around to a painful
state of consciousness. His skull throbbed as he lay on his side, while
tight ropes held his hands behind his back. Ameny could hear raspy
breathing and coughing in the lightless space as if others were close
by.*

*There was the sound of voices. Ameny's eyes adjusted to the dark,
and he could now see that he had been dragged into the acolytes'
chamber, along with several others. Senusret's plan—whatever it
was—had been hatched.*

*Excited and forceful, voices drifted from under the chamber door's
threshold. Something was about to happen, possibly a rite of sacrifice.*

*The agitated voices faded away, followed by footsteps, which grew
quiet. Someone groaned in pain not far from Ameny; the man may
have been badly wounded in the fighting that had spilled through
the temple's halls on this ill-fortuned night.*

*In the darkness, the door to the chamber creaked as it opened just
slightly. A temple cat squeezed in, its paws padding across the stone
floor to where Ameny had been lain, a prisoner of the betrayers.*

*The cat leaped onto the top of Ameny's arm and peered down at
him, its large, almond-shaped eyes bright and gleaming in the dark.
Dropping behind his back, the cat began to gnaw at the rope binding
Ameny's wrists, working quickly and with purpose.*

Soon, the rope loosened, its abrasive fibers no longer cutting into the novitiate scribe's now tender flesh. Pulling the rope apart, Ameny cautiously freed himself, furtively bringing both arms forward. Nonetheless, he continued to lie against his side, not knowing who else might be in the room with him.

Its work done, the cat stealthily returned to the chamber's door, slipping back out into the hallway in silence. Ameny decided to wait until he was sure no one would raise an alarm before trying to escape.

Even so, *Ameny considered,* someone might spy me in the hall as I exit the acolyte's chamber. Is the entire temple in thrall, captives of the subverters? *He prayed to Bastet that others were still free and strenuously resisting.*

From the prone bodies around him came shallow, fitful breathing, but no one seemed to be aware of or watching him. Ameny let the last strands of rope fall from his wrists and crouched in place in preparation for his escape. He crawled toward the ajar door and pushed his head out into the hallway, praying not to be seen.

There was no light, and no sentry seemed to be there. Why had those captured been left unguarded?

From somewhere in the temple, there came rhythmic chanting, voices calling out in a long-forgotten dialect of the Old Kingdom. Ameny crept through the darkness, following the sound of the chants and then the light from torches to the once-towering statue of Bastet, positioned at the center of the temple's columnated outermost hall.

The statue of the Goddess had been desecrated, its alabaster stones smashed and scattered, a partial ring of priests and acolytes prostrating in obeisance around its broken pedestal. High Priest Senusret stood before this treacherous half-circle, his arms raised toward what remained of Bastet's consecrated effigy. He lowered his arms and, at once, the apostates' blasphemous intonations ceased. Senusret then spoke, still facing away from the others.

"The servants of Bastet have been vanquished and will soon be but bloodied offerings to our Great Mother, the Night Queen," Senusret pronounced, his baritone voice echoing in the now quiescent temple. "With this first sacrifice of the fool Minhotep, our Mother will begin to take form in the Waking World. With more, She will finally be free to resume Her reign among mortal men, no longer trapped by Bastet in the Land of Dream. Only offerings of Bastet's anointed can redeem our Mistress."

From his place of concealment among the pillars, Ameny then noticed a bound and gagged Minhotep lying not far from Senusret, his face battered but unmistakable in the lucent torchlight.

Reaching into his robes, Senusret revealed an ornamental dagger of a kind Ameny had never seen. Senusret then pointed at Minhotep and commanded, "Bring him to the foot of the idol, and let us prepare for the arrival of our Great Mother."

Dragged by the priest Senbi and an acolyte, Minhotep was laid near Senusret, the high priest posturing over him triumphantly. Ameny turned away from the grotesque scene and saw many temple cats gathering among the pillars behind him. He then spied even more in the shadows of the pillars opposite him, their keen eyes glinting in anticipation. Dozens of Bastet's hallowed cats encircled the traitors, perhaps more.

Shrieking in an alien language, Senusret gripped the sloping dagger's hilt above his head as a dark figure took shape over the base of Bastet's vandalized statute. The amorphous shadow coalesced, beginning to resemble the contours of a woman, her hips wide and her hair flowing.

Senusret rolled an unconscious Minhotep onto his back and readied his sacrificial blade, still calling out the ritual's incantation. The chief scribe of Bastet would be an oblation to the demoness, this otherworldly interloper from outside time and space, who had long been imprisoned by the goddess of cats in the Land of Dream.

"Stop, Senusret! You betrayer, you weak-willed servant of your own mortal ambition! Bastet will have Her revenge at this mo-

ment." Ameny stepped out from the shadows, confronting Senusret and his prostrate minions. This was the distraction the temple cats needed.

A cat hissed and then pounced. Its claws out, the cat leaped onto Senusret's face as he turned his head in surprise at Ameny's unforeseen intrusion. Senusret screamed as the ferocious temple cat tore into him, blood flowing onto his robes. More cats jumped onto Senusret's shoulders as he flailed about, clawing his eyes and blinding the Night Queen's servitor in the Waking World.

The priests and acolytes rose to their feet in fear, terrified in the presence of Bastet's divine wrath, as the shadowy form of the woman on the pedestal wavered and began to fade. The ritual of opening a gate into Bastet's temple had been broken, its summoner collapsing to the floor under the fierce onslaught of Bastet's most beloved.

The traitorous clerics fled, running from the temple and out into the moonless night, the unforgiving desert lands waiting for them. They could never again return to the place they had forsaken, having betrayed their sacred oath to their goddess, the Great Mother of Cats.

"What was that I just saw?" Felix asked Sophia, blinking as the vision in the crystal ball slowly evaporated. He then looked directly at her from across the table. "Did a see a real past?"

"I can't say," Sophia replied calmly. "I'm not even certain we had the same vision. What the ball shows me often differs from what my guests see."

Sophia's cat sat near Felix, looking up at him from its spot on a heavily embroidered rug near his chair. The cat purred as if satisfied by something. Sophia shuffled the cards in her deck again and laid them on the table.

"Please choose another card," Sophia requested. "Which one draws you this time?" she asked Felix, her voice hopeful.

Felix's eyes scanned the intricate design on the back of each card, the faces of the cards hidden from him. He selected a card from the far-right end of the spread and then turned it over so Sophia could view its face. The card was upside down.

"The Magician," Sophia announced hesitantly, perhaps surprised by a reversed card drawn from the deck. The face of the card showed a man dressed in the garb of an alchemist or a sorcerer, evidently engaged in occult practice.

"Is that bad?" Felix asked, probing and anxious. "You seem uncomfortable suddenly."

Sophia replied, "The card can be interpreted in many ways. When the Magician card appears reversed, it can mean you or someone else is not on the right path. It can also be a warning that someone may be trying to deceive or manipulate you. But I can't say right now. Let's gaze into the ball again and look for some answers."

The Magician Card—A Present

"You didn't tell me you had a cat!" Celeste exclaimed, dismayed by the sight of a marmalade-hued tabby gazing up at her from the throw rug where she stood. "Can't you put it outside? At least until it's dark?"

Celeste's mother smiled and took her daughter's winter coat, which she then hung in the entryway closet. "Of course, my dear," she said, her pleasure at seeing Celeste again distracting her from her daughter's curious reaction to the family cat. "He'll crawl into the garage until I let him back in. We adopted Ramses just this spring. He's a rescue from a local shelter."

Mother reached down to pick him up, but the cat dashed past her and Celeste, heading outside through the open front door. As Mother pushed the door shut, a cold gust of wind blew into the house, the icy draft spent almost as soon as it came.

Walking into the kitchen, Mother revealed, "We're having glazed ham and casserole. I hope you're hungry. Felix and your father can only eat so much."

Sitting on the living room sofa, Celeste watched her father watch television. She was unsure when her brother would return from his shopping errands, though dinner was soon. The siblings were visiting their parents for the holidays and hadn't seen one another in some time.

Even though he had arrived before Celeste, Felix had seemed pressed to leave once the celebratory observances were over. A nervous gloom hung over him; Celeste noted Felix was mostly anxious and untalkative during their brief interactions. He had begun telling her but hurriedly left "to buy presents" instead.

When asked what was wrong, Felix had confided in Celeste that he'd been having bad dreams lately. He'd been having trouble sleeping, and the dreams he'd been having were "possibly real," as if they weren't dreams at all but something else. Felix had said this almost as an aside, out of earshot of their mother and father.

But then he'd insisted that he no longer wanted to talk about it, that it was nothing, and that it should pass soon anyway. Celeste had decided she wouldn't bring up the dreams again unless Felix wanted to discuss them with her. She watched through the living room's bay window as Felix's car pulled into the driveway. Her brother got out, store-wrapped boxes in his arms.

Celeste sat at the oval dining room table with their mother and father, across from Felix. Mother sliced a serving of ham and put it on a dinner plate, handing the dish to Felix, who accepted it without a word. He had been very quiet since returning from his shopping trip but had at least said he'd found everything he was looking for.

Mother smiled and said, "You should be able to get a good night's rest after dinner, Felix." She quietly studied her son as he ate his Christmas ham. "I thought I heard you get up in the middle of the night last night. Were you having trouble sleeping?"

"That's funny," commented Felix, briefly puzzled. "I don't remember waking up, let alone getting out of bed. Are you sure it was me?"

Still smiling but now guarded, Mother replied, "Yes, dear, I heard your door open and footsteps in the hall. It could have only been you. You could be a sleepwalker but don't realize it. You might need to get checked if it becomes a problem."

Felix shrugged dismissively and went back to eating his dinner. Father had watched the exchange without comment, eating slowly before finally leaving the dining room, not bothering to excuse himself.

Observing Father askance as he made his way to the living room to watch more television, Mother turned to Celeste and inquired about the strangely exotic pendant she was wearing. The glossy pendant, which hung over Celeste's blouse, was very noticeable, its set stone smooth and black.

"What's that around your neck, Celeste?" Mother queried with another smile, genuinely curious about the unusual piece. "You've never worn it before. And it's not at all like your usual style of accessory. Did you find it in some old collection?"

"This?" Celeste answered in surprise, glancing down at the round obsidian stone hanging from a silver chain around her neck, its shape that of the moon, dark within dark. "Oh, a long-lost friend from my school days gave it to me as a gift. She travels extensively and acquired it overseas. She said someone wanted me to have it."

Felix thought for a moment that the pendant's stone must represent the new moon—when the Earth's only natural satellite moved through the night sky unseen. Tonight was one such night, the sky outside already dark and twilit.

Felix got into bed and shut off the bedside lamp, having already brushed his teeth. He had the guest bedroom to himself as Celeste was sleeping in her former bedroom, which had been kept mostly the same since she had moved out years ago.

Felix was the younger sibling but had left home earlier than his sister, and his bedroom had been turned into a guest room in his absence. The bedroom was now spartan and unadorned, with only a bed and some other basic furniture. A reading lamp stood on the nightstand.

Even with the curtains pulled back from the room's solitary window, it was very dark, the overcast day having turned into a nearly starless night. Hugging his pillow and burying his head into its firm softness, Felix dozed but couldn't fall asleep.

He rolled onto his side, searching for comfort, hoping for a dreamless rest. Should I tell Celeste more about the dreams in the morning? *Felix thought, the quiet stillness of the room nearly suffocating.* I don't want to sound crazy. But it's like I'm seeing into someone's past when I dream. I see things I've never known about before, terrible things. And others could be nightmares of the future.

A gust of wind rattled the bedroom window's frame. Someone was sitting in the chair near the closet door. Felix sat up in bed with a start and peered at the mysterious figure, its dim outline the only thing visible. It was a woman, watching him from where she sat.

"Celeste?" Felix whispered hoarsely as his heavy-lidded eyes adjusted to the near darkness. "What are you doing in my room? Go to sleep."

The figure said nothing for a moment but then began to speak. "Those dreams you've been having, they aren't dreams. They're visions. Visions of both the past and the future. I've been sending them to you, weakening your defenses, getting you ready." The voice sounded like Celeste's but had a subtly menacing tinge.

Pushing himself upright, Felix put his bare feet on the bedroom floor. "Celeste, I'm tired," Felix mumbled wearily as he continued to observe the figure. "If this is a joke, I don't appreciate the humor. Go back to bed and let me be. I need to sleep."

"Your sister betrayed you," the figure continued, rising from its chair. "She begged, pleading that I spare her and take you instead. So, I shall."

As Felix began to stand, the figure lunged, rushing across the room and then swallowing him wholly into the soul-nullifying abyss of its dark embrace.

Shaken, Felix looked away from the crystal ball. Sophia stared at him intensely as if she had been watching his emotions play out as the ball had divulged its secrets. Pushing himself away from the table, Felix drew a deep breath and looked at Sophia with spent eyes.

"The ball showed me a recent memory this time. From a few days ago," he explained, speaking between terse, jagged breaths as he fought to compose himself. "But not how I remembered it. Someone came to visit me in my room at my parents' house. I thought it was just a dream. One of my more terrifying nightmares, even. But it seemed to have really happened."

"I saw nothing," Sophia replied, her eyes watchful and vigilant as if expecting danger. "Only the swirling mists. Whatever the ball chose to reveal to you was hidden from me."

Sophia's cat made a low, rumbling purr, almost a growl. Then, darting behind a plush armchair, the cat vanished out of sight again.

"There's a final card, isn't there?" Felix asked Sophia, nervous and expectant. "A card that will show my future? Let's draw it and see."

"Your future or a future, as I said." Sophia shuffled the cards a final time and then spread them out, face down, before Felix. She didn't look at him but instead watched in anticipation for the last card to be drawn by the querent.

Felix pulled from near the center of the deck. He turned the card over and saw a regal woman seated on a splendid throne, her head bejeweled with a golden crown.

"The Empress," Sophia uttered, her voice dead. Then, almost whispering, she said, "She's come for me."

"What? Who's come for you?" Felix asked, despite his fear of the answer. "What does the card mean?"

Distracted, as if she had been snapped out of a momentary trance, Sophia gave her interpretation. "This card represents power and dominion; the woman holds a scepter as a symbol of her authority. This authority is feminine and can be divine in nature."

"Divine and feminine?" Felix asked. "A goddess?"

"Stare into the ball this one last time," Sophia requested, her voice distant and dreamlike. "You or I will see a future. But be warned. What you see may not be pleasant."

The hazy gray mists within the ball swirled again, and the contours of a metropolis began to form. Only... it was desolate, without life. A dead husk resting on what was once a living world...

The Empress Card—A Future

Eternally howling winds swept over a barren landscape, the destroyed and desiccated remains of a great city littering the gutted terrain. Churning like an inky ocean caught within a swirling maelstrom, the sunless skies utterly obscured any sign of light beyond them, casting doubt upon even the existence of the heavens.

Flashes of sick-orange lightning interspersed the black velvet of the dark, roiling clouds and, in this turbulent welkin, a vast whirling vortex fixated itself over a necropolitan temple of gargantuan black stones. The few survivors hid themselves, wallowing in mortal fear, terrified of She who had wrought this earth-shattering apocalypse upon mankind. She now hunted them, seeking the final repose of these last remnants of humanity.

"She would only come out at night before, when it first started," a woman confided, a bitter cough emerging from her dry throat after she spoke. "But now, it's always night. A perpetual night without end. Now She comes out whenever She wants to."

A man huddled against the wall of the small, dilapidated shelter, drinking from the cup the woman had given him. Ragged and dirty, he shivered and breathed in raspy gulps; so little warmth came from the crackling fire in the pit at his feet.

"We're in a place where She can't easily find us, though," the woman continued, watching the man drink the last drop from his cup. "This place was a holy place; I think they called it a 'cathedral' before She came. So, it's not visible to the Night Queen. God still protects us, even though He seems to have forsaken all."

"The Night Queen?" the man replied, putting down his cup. "How do you know She's called that? The others called Her a demon or just a monster."

The woman pulled her frayed head wrapping tighter and sat across from the man. "I can hear the chanting from that horrible stone place," she replied, her eyes widening inordinately as she recalled the ghastly chants. "Her worshippers pray to Her; sometimes, I understand what they say."

"How can you hear anything above that wind?" the man retorted. "It never ends and only gets louder. If it keeps up, I don't know if I'll ever be able to sleep again."

"I can sometimes hear the chants in my sleep," the woman said quietly. "There's no one here now, so I sleep alone. The others were all taken."

Above the winds, there was a metal clanging outside the shelter. The woman stood alert and ready, reaching for her crossbow. The taut string tied to pots and pans the woman set as an alarm had been tripped again after the man had blundered into it earlier.

The woman said, "Wait here. I'll see what it might be. Another refugee, maybe, to bring our numbers to three."

Slipping through the crude wood door of the makeshift shelter, the woman stepped out into the collapsed edifice of what had once been a Gothic cathedral, the ruins of its marble walls and vaulted ceiling hinting at the blasted basilica's vanished grandeur.

The clangor of a metal pot echoed again as the woman approached the site of her trap. Someone started to run. "Stop," the woman called out. "Don't move. I'm armed. If you don't stop and turn around, I'll shoot."

In the darkness of the ruined church, the intruder paused and held up her arms as if to surrender. She turned and faced her captor.

"I'm Celeste," the woman said, trembling. "Please don't shoot. I was only looking for somewhere to sleep. I'm so cold and hungry. Please, just let me stay here and rest for a while."

The woman lowered her crossbow and carefully studied her guest. She was older, close to middle-aged, but not haggard and starved like all the other survivors she'd encountered. This was someone who had lived in comfort and eaten regular meals until only recently.

"Come here and stand next to me," the woman ordered sharply. "Keep your hands up. I'm going to search you for weapons."

Celeste did as she was told and the woman looked for a knife or anything else that could cause harm on the woman's person. Her garments and coat were new and had only recently become torn, not yet the tatters everyone else wore.

"OK, you're fine," the woman said as she finished her inspection. "I can take you back to my shelter. But let's go; it's not safe here, exposed to the open skies."

The door to the shelter buckled open with a push and Celeste followed the woman inside. The man was asleep near the firepit, its smoldering pile of kindling nearly spent.

"I collected him today, too," the woman told Celeste, gesturing at the sleeping man. "I don't know much about him, but he may never

wake up again. Every day, the air gets harder to breathe, and he didn't sound so good. But I'm going to relight the fire."

Celeste sat on the ground near the man and listened to his slow, shallow breaths. The fire pit lit up as fresh kindling burned, providing light and heat in the dark, cramped space.

The woman took a small box from a rickety shelf and put it between her and Celeste. "I don't have much food, but I'll share what I've got. It's getting harder to scavenge now that there's never any daytime. Here, eat up."

Pulling back the box's lid, Celeste saw it was full of brown plastic wrappers, each about the width of her palm. She took out one and started to tear it open.

"I found these in the back of a truck outside a supermarket," the woman told Celeste. "The place had been picked clean, but this box was under one of the seats. They're probably stale, but I didn't get sick when I ate them, so you'll be fine."

Celeste took a bite. It was a cookie, something like oatmeal. She said, "I haven't had anything like this in so long," as she munched hungrily on her treat. "Thank you so much."

The woman said nothing in reply, examining Celeste cautiously in the light of the fire as she ate. Where did she come from? *the woman thought, noting her guest's age and lack of the marks of hardship.* How could she have survived this long without others? *Then she saw it.*

"What's that on your hand?" the woman asked, suddenly afraid.

Celeste paused and was silent.

"It's Her sign, isn't it?" the woman insisted, panicked now, pointing to the crescent moon above an inverted cross branded on the skin between Celeste's thumb and index finger. "You're from the stone place, aren't you?"

Celeste rose to her feet as the winds outside grew steadily into a tumultuous roar, drowning out the possibility of any more words between herself and her host. Above the cacophony, fiercely beating leathery wings could be heard as something landed on the planks of the shelter's roof. There was a thumping sound as the visitor moved above them, followed by cracking and splintering as the roof was torn off in pieces.

The woman screamed, barely a whimper in the deafening winds that swept in and battered her and Celeste. She pressed her hands to her ears, trying to block out the din of the never-ending gale, as a horror from a time before mankind hovered above them, both majestic and infernal in its aspect.

As the unrelenting winds assailed her, Celeste moved to escape but was snatched by the clawed hands of her mistress, the Night Queen.

Cowering in the dark, the fire pit having been extinguished, the woman saw two eyes that burned like flaming coals within a visage that was both human and inhuman.

The Night Queen pulled Herself aloft, Celeste firmly in Her grasp. Shrieking and cursing in some ancient and obscene tongue, Celeste was dragged skyward, the last echoes of her curses dying as the terrible winds retreated. The errant priestess would soon suffer the furious wrath of her goddess, now the absolute ruler of what had once been the realm of Man.

"Did you see it? What's going to happen?" Felix panted, his mouth slack, his forehead beaded and feverish after glimpsing this vision of a horrific end times.

"Yes, this time I did," replied Sophia. "But who's that behind you?"

Felix turned his head to glance over his shoulder and then stopped.

A woman, decaying and leprous, stood at the back of his chair. Her putrid, worm-eaten face oozed a black ichor. The room at once suffused with the stench of a charnel house; it was as if a mass grave had been opened, its rotting carcasses spilling forth. But, in all this ghastliness, the woman's eyes stood as her most terrifying facet. They were blood-red and glowed with the flickering fires of Hades itself.

Felix's lifeless body slumped forward onto the table, rapidly becoming a moldering and decomposing corpse. The fresh roses in the hanging wall vase wilted preternaturally until their falling petals crumbled as bistre-colored soot to the parlor floor below. The air was thin and acrid, suggesting more than a trace of sulfur. There was now nothing but blackness, the day having vanished in mere moments. An ominous rumbling from all directions permeated the umbral dark in which the room had become enshrouded.

"I knew you were coming," Sophia told the woman from her chair, the being's burning eyes the only visible thing in the room. "I knew when I couldn't see his vision of the present, and then with certainty after he pulled the last card from my deck. You were able to take possession of that boy and enter here, evading my wards and spells of protection. Well played."

The woman answered in a terrible, hissing voice. "I will be free, Sophia," She proclaimed, gloating and exultant. "As Bastet's servant, you are the way, and I will be free. You are ensnared and will be my gate into Waking World, where I will resume my rightful place of power. There is no other path for you."

"But there is," Sophia answered, calm and resolute. "The blessings of my goddess, the Great Mother of Cats, preserves me. I call on you, Mother Bastet. It is you who are trapped, Lilith. You will return to the desolation of your imprisonment, forever."

The spotted silver-gray cat revealed itself, draped in a gauzy shroud of pure light. Lilith saw the cat and screamed, an unholy shriek from the unfathomable depths of the Abyss; she then became transfixed in an instant, muted.

Moving with ease and grace, the cat came forward on velvet paws and sat at Her ancient adversary's feet. She delicately licked Her paw, not budging from the spot, as the dazzling light surrounding Her became more brilliant with each passing moment.

Bastet's intense healing luminance filled the space until the darkness was pushed back, the demoness growing more distant until the rays of the sun returned—and, with the cleansing sun, the demoness banished. The parlor room now stood empty save for the wise clairvoyant and her cat.

Sophia reached down and gently picked up her cat, cradling Her in her lap. She stroked the cat's sleek fur, softly saying in a language long dead, "I am your beloved, my queen, for now and for all time."

About the Author

James Dermond is a writer who lives in Colorado. Intrigued from an early age by horror anthologies and the short story form, he offers this book as his latest modest contribution to the genre.

Doorways to the Unseen 5: 6 Tales of Terror and Suspense is the fifth volume in a series of short story collections. The sixth volume in the series will be published in April 2023.

To sign up for free eBooks and other future giveaways, please subscribe to James Dermond's author website here:

www.jamesdermond.com

James Dermond's Amazon Author Page

https://www.amazon.com/James-Dermond/e/B01M1S54YP

James Dermond's Goodreads Author Page

https://www.goodreads.com/author/show/15862747.James_Dermond

James Dermond on Facebook

https://www.facebook.com/JamesDermondAuthor/

James Dermond on Twitter

https://twitter.com/JamesDermond

Postscript

Thank you for reading the latest volume of the short horror story series Doorways to the Unseen! This book is the fifth in what will eventually become a twelve-volume series. Ambages Books plans to release two volumes each year, with the final volume scheduled for publication in April 2026. Following that, a multi-volume hardcover edition of the collected stories will be available in October of the same year.

If you enjoyed this collection of stories, please leave a review on Amazon and other online bookstores where volumes in the Doorways to the Unseen series can be found. A positive review will help promote the book and inform other readers of the book's merits.